"You're willing to walk away from this?"

Emily forced the words out, unsure if she really wanted to hear the answer. Her heart hammered in her throat, and she met Greg's gaze.

"Walk away?" He shook his head and his eyes met hers, snapping in irritation. "Do I look like I'm walking away to you?"

He was angry now, too, and she could feel the tension in the room mounting. She'd rather face him angry than keep butting her head up against his self-controlled calm.

"Then what are you doing?" she demanded.

He dropped his arms and stepped toward her. He pinned her with those fierce blue eyes, emotions battling over his rugged features. "I'm trying really, really hard not to fall head over heels in love with you, Emily. That's what I'm doing."

"And how is that working out for you?" she asked, lifting her chin in defiance.

His answer was a last step toward her, his strong arm sliding around her waist and pulling her close to him so that she could feel the steady beat of his heart.

PATRICIA JOHNS

willfully became a starving artist after she finished her BA in English literature. It was all right, because she was single, attractive and had a family to back her up "just in case." She lived in a tiny room in the downtown core of a city, worked sundry part-time jobs to keep herself fed and wrote the first novel she would have published.

That was over ten years ago, and in the meantime, she's had another ten novels published. This book is her first for Love Inspired, and her dedication to the written word hasn't diminished.

She's married, has a young son and a small bird named Frankie. She couldn't be happier.

His Unexpected Family

Patricia Johns

Recycling programs for this product may not exist in your area.

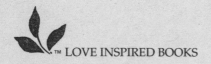

™ LOVE INSPIRED BOOKS

ISBN-13: 978-0-373-87828-4

HIS UNEXPECTED FAMILY

This edition published by arrangement with Love Inspired Books.

® and TM are trademarks of Love Inspired Books, used under license. Trademarks indicated with ® are registered in the United States Patent and Trademark Office, the Canadian Trade Marks Office and in other countries.

www.LoveInspiredBooks.com

Printed in U.S.A.

The Lord your God is with you,
the Mighty Warrior who saves.
He will take great delight in you;
in His love He will no longer rebuke you,
but will rejoice over you with singing.
—*Zephaniah* 3:17

To my mom, who raised a writer

Chapter One

Emily was expecting a baby. In fact, she was expecting the little one to arrive that very afternoon, and every car that passed by on the road outside made her look up. She attempted to keep herself occupied by sorting through the boxes of decorations she'd taken from her kindergarten classroom the week before, but the distraction wasn't working terribly well.

Emily looked down at the laminated cards with big, colorful letters printed across them. As she absently arranged them and tucked them into an envelope to be used in September, her eyes flickered back toward the window. Her plan had been to get as much work out of the way as she could before little Cora arrived, but perhaps that had been overly ambitious. Pulling her dark waves away from her face with one hand, she dropped the envelope on top of a box of art supplies.

The crunch of tires on her gravel drive made her look up again, her eyes trained out the window. A police cruiser eased behind her SUV, and before the driver's-side door even opened, Emily pushed herself out of her seat and went to open the front door.

The police officer faced away from her as he leaned

into the backseat. Broad shoulders tapered down to a strong back, and she half expected him to lift some heavy weight from the car. But then he straightened and turned toward her, a baby car seat in one hand, his steel-blue eyes moving over her matter-of-factly.

"Miss Shaw?" he said.

"Hi," Emily said. "Yes, that's me."

"Sorry I'm late." He walked across the last of the drive to the shade of her front door. His biceps flexed under the weight of the car seat, and he gave her a professional smile. "It's nice to meet you in person. I'm Chief Greg Taylor. We spoke on the phone."

"Yes, yes, absolutely." She stepped back to let him inside, and as he passed her, his arm brushing hers, she could just detect the musk of his cologne.

He was better-looking than she'd given him credit for during their telephone conversation. With close-cropped blond hair, going just a tiny bit gray at the temples, he had a calm and collected look about him. His blue eyes seemed to take in every detail as his gaze swung around the room. He placed the car seat on the couch, and Emily moved closer to the little bundle, bending down to peek at the tiny face.

The baby was sleeping, a baby girl so tiny that Emily was almost afraid to touch her. She had a downy frosting of red hair on top of her head, and her skin was so pale that Emily thought she was nearly translucent. The little thing lay there in the car seat, her small pink tongue sticking out in her sleep, and Emily let out a soft sigh.

"There she is." Emily touched one little hand, feeling the baby-soft skin. When she looked up, she saw Chief Taylor watching her thoughtfully.

"I'm sorry about your cousin." He pressed his lips together. "Were you close?"

"Not really." Emily felt slight embarrassment flush her cheeks. "I didn't know she trusted me this much... you know, leaving me as guardian in her will."

"How long since you saw her last?" he asked.

"Years...maybe five or six?" Emily tried to recall the last time she and her cousin had been in the same room. It had been some sort of family reunion, and she was pretty sure it was the time that one of her uncles broke his leg falling off the porch.

"She obviously thought a lot of you."

Emily nodded. "She was quite private. I mean, we were Facebook friends, but she didn't really post anything. I didn't know much about what was going on with her."

"It's understandable." He gave her a sympathetic smile and made a couple of notes on a pad of paper.

"I didn't know she was pregnant," Emily added. "She didn't tell anyone." She looked back down at the tiny baby and shook her head sadly. "But looking at Baby Cora, there is no denying who her mother was."

Emily bent down and unbuckled the harness. Cora wriggled as Emily slid a hand under her little rump and lifted her out of the car seat. The infant nestled into Emily's arms, snuggling close, and she felt a wave of tenderness for the tiny thing.

"Are you going to be all right?" he asked. "Do you need social services to come give you a hand with anything?"

"Social services?" Emily laughed softly. "Do we even have social services in Haggerston?"

"Well, *social services* consists mostly of Madge Middleton. She's a foster mom who gives some pretty sound advice." He shot her a wry grin.

"My mother would be insulted. Don't you worry

about me. I have a big family with lots of women just waiting to tell me exactly how to do things."

"Good." He seemed to relax. "You'll be fine, then. I probably know some of your family."

"In a place this size, it's hard not to." She laughed. "You graduated high school a few years before me."

"Really?" He eyed her with an amused look. "Are you related to Steve Shaw, by any chance?"

"My cousin."

"Well, now I'm going to have to root out my old yearbook." He chuckled softly, the sound oddly comforting.

"Oh, don't. Ninth grade wasn't graceful." Emily rolled her eyes. "Trust me. I was entirely forgettable."

He gave a slow smile and tapped his notebook with a nub of a pencil. "Can I see your ID?"

"My ID?"

"Policy. I've got to make sure you are who I think you are before I leave a baby with you."

"Oh, of course…" She blushed and headed to the kitchen to grab her wallet. While she rummaged through her bag, she mentally chastised herself. He was here on business, not here to flirt with her. Finding her wallet with one hand and holding the baby in the other, she came back to the living room, determined to be nothing but professional herself.

"How are you doing for baby things?" he asked while he looked over her ID.

"I think I'm all right."

"The officers at the station brought in a few things from home, if you're interested," he said, raising his eyes from her driver's license and meeting hers with a steady gaze that made her cheeks feel warm. "The officers who have kids, that is."

"Oh, that's really nice," she said. "Thanks."

"Should I drop them by tomorrow, then?"

"Yes, thanks. I really appreciate this, Chief. Thank them for me."

Chief Taylor handed her back her license and gave her a formal smile. "Take care. I'll see you tomorrow."

"Tomorrow."

With that, Greg Taylor, the handsome chief of police of Haggerston, Montana, trotted down her front steps and got back into the squad car. Emily looked down at the sleeping baby in her arms. Cora's little hands lay limply across her chest, and she let out a deep sigh in her sleep. She was a beautiful little thing, and looking down at her, she felt an involuntary wave of love.

Oh, Lord, she prayed silently. *Is this real? Is she really going to be mine?*

As she watched Greg's car pull out of her drive and disappear, she smelled something, and she laughed softly to herself. Well, one thing was very real tonight, and it was this diaper. It looked as though things were just beginning!

As Chief Greg Taylor walked back into the Haggerston Police Station, he stifled a yawn. It had been a long day, to say the least, and as he strode through the town's small station, the officers he passed glanced up and gave him polite nods. The station always looked busy, with telephones ringing, officers coming and going and the general hubbub that came with twenty-odd people focused on their own work. It might not be considered much compared to a city station, but for a place the size of Haggerston, it was something. It might look like chaos to an untrained eye, but to Chief Taylor, who had spent his entire adult career as a cop, it was a smoothly oiled machine…or at least as oiled as discipline, training and several gallons of coffee could make it.

"Hey, Chief!" A sergeant waved a file at him. "Some paperwork from that 11-80 the other day. You want it on your desk?"

"I'll take it." Chief Taylor grabbed the file on his way by and headed around the desks toward his office at the far side of the station. He tossed the file on his desk and swung the door shut behind him. He stood in the relative quiet and glanced at his watch. Picking up the phone, he dialed the number to the Shady Pines Nursing Home.

"Shady Pines," the nurse's voice sang.

"Hi, this is Chief Taylor. I'm just wondering how my mother is doing."

"Hi, Chief, this is Fran. Your mom had quite a good day. She had her favorite dinner tonight—Salisbury steak."

"Oh, good." He felt the smile come to his lips. "And how is she…otherwise?"

"She's been confused." Sympathy entered the nurse's tone. "She wouldn't let us bathe her today, but we're hoping that by later this evening, she'll be calmer. Sometimes evening routines have a more relaxing effect on her."

Greg ran a hand through his hair. "Do you need me to come by?"

"You're always welcome, Chief, but she's been very wary around men again today. I'm not sure it would do much good."

He nodded, more to himself than to the nurse on the other end of the call. "Well, keep me posted. I'll call back later."

"Absolutely, Chief. You have a good evening."

He hung up the phone and picked up the file on his

desk. His shift had been over for two hours already, but for some reason he couldn't bring himself to go home. His mind was still on that 11-80.

11-80. It was easier to refer to it numerically than to voice the reality of the situation. It had been a terrible car accident with crumpled metal, leaking fuel and a gravely injured driver. The semitruck that hit the little car was relatively unharmed, and the truck driver was incredibly shaken, but in one piece, which was more than could be said for the occupant of the car. He tried to push the mental images out of his head, but the one that remained was the pleading face of the injured mother, her face covered in blood and her eyes filled with fear.

"Her name is Emily Shaw. She's Cora's godmother. You have to call her. Please. I don't want my baby with a stranger. You have to call her!"

He'd sworn that he would, and there was something about that young mother's intensity, her insistence that he take care of this, that stuck with him. Fourteen hours later, that little baby became an orphan when her mother succumbed to her injuries and passed away in the E.R., and the least he could do was fulfill that frightened mother's last wishes and personally bring the baby to Emily Shaw. Which he had done this afternoon. The baby was now settled with her godmother. Job complete, right?

So why couldn't he let it go? Why was Emily's face now swimming in his mind, too?

But the image of Emily Shaw, with her dark, wavy hair and her sparkling eyes, didn't bring up the same anxiety and guilt that the other images did. A young, dying mother, terrified for her baby. His own mother, suffering from Alzheimer's, unaware of who he was. A tiny infant, orphaned by a fatal accident. Yet there was something comforting in that calm kindergarten teacher with her disheveled papers and self-deprecating laugh. While he knew that his professional position didn't make a personal relationship with her very appropriate, thinking about Emily Shaw was infinitely more pleasant than the other options.

He'd pick up those baby things the officers had collected and bring them by. Maybe that would tie up this case in his head and let him move on.

Chapter Two

The next afternoon, Greg pulled into Emily's drive in his unmarked squad car and parked. He sat motionless for a moment or two, listening to the background noise of voices on the police radio. Apparently, there was a 10-33—a triggered security alarm—from a locked store. Across town another officer was taking a Code 8—a restroom break. Like most things, that just sounded better in a numerical code than to state the obvious. Greg's thoughts weren't on the voices, however. He found himself feeling somewhat nervous, something he didn't feel very often. He took a deep breath and opened the car door.

Emily's home sprawled just south of the small community of Haggerston. A bungalow-style rancher, it had a large yard hemmed in by a log fence. The effect was quite rustic, and he liked it. The well-maintained yard sported flower beds arranged naturally, as if little patches of flowers and leafy plants had just decided to push up around a rock or a tree, although in Montana, that sort of natural sprouting rarely happened without a good deal of loving care. Her front door had a woven twig wreath hanging on it, and he imagined that come the holiday season, it would be festooned with berries and holly. Her windows were covered with shuttered blinds that were open at the moment, letting the summer light in and keeping prying eyes out. As a police officer, he approved of her use of privacy.

In the trunk, Greg had several bags and boxes of baby things he'd picked up from the station, and he carried them to her front door before ringing the bell. He didn't hear anything for a few moments, and he was about to ring again when he heard the sound of footfalls. Her peephole darkened for a moment. Then the lock scraped, and she pulled the door open.

Emily stood in the doorway, her hair still damp from a shower, wearing a pair of jeans and a loose, pink blouse that brought out the color in her cheeks. Her hair had left wet patches on her shoulders, and her face was makeup free. She looked fresh, albeit a little tired, the warm June breeze tugging at some wisps of hair around her face that were drying faster than the rest.

"Hi." She angled her head to gesture him inside. "Wow, that's a lot of boxes."

He looked at the pile next to the door and nodded his agreement.

"I've been assured that all of it is absolutely necessary," he said. "I took their word for it."

She smiled, her eyes meeting his with a sparkle of amusement. "I hope this isn't too far out of your way."

"We've all taken a personal interest in Cora." He gave Emily a shrug. "And you're her new mom."

"Well…" A glimmer of something crossed her face, and she made a concerted effort to mask it. "I'm hoping, at least. I've heard that these things can be a bit complicated."

Greg nodded. It was true, and he wasn't one to give

false reassurances. Custody cases could be incredibly complicated, and no one could say what would happen with this one. Instead of answering her, he put his attention into bringing the rest of the boxes inside, piling them neatly inside the door.

"How is everything going with Cora?" he asked instead.

"Surprisingly well, considering how little I slept last night." She gave him a wry smile. He had to admit, she looked pretty good for not having slept, but then, he probably wasn't noticing the same things she was. Emily Shaw seemed like the kind of woman who could look pretty good wearing a paper bag.

"Well, this is it." He nodded toward the boxes. "This should help get you started."

"Are you on the clock?" she asked.

"Not officially, ma'am."

"Did you want to come in for a cup of iced tea or something?"

Greg cleared his throat. He hadn't come over to shoot the breeze, but he had to admit that the prospect of an iced tea on a hot day with some beautiful company appealed.

"Unless you're busy—" She blushed.

"Well, I suppose a few minutes wouldn't hurt."

Emily rewarded him with a brilliant smile and angled her head into the house.

"Come to the kitchen. We'll be more comfortable there."

Greg followed Emily through a cool, spacious living room into the kitchen. It was lined with bright windows opening up onto a large veranda out back. The kitchen was a cook's dream, with polished black appliances, a gorgeous amount of counter space and an island in the middle with a selection of stainless-steel pots hanging above.

Next to a small kitchen table by a window sat a little bassinet, baby Cora nestled under a light knitted blanket, snoring softly. Emily peeked in on her, pausing for a moment on her way to the refrigerator.

"So you were friends with Steve, were you?" she asked, glancing over her shoulder.

"*Friends* might be a strong word. I knew him." Greg perched on the edge of a stool by the counter, grateful for a topic of conversation that didn't involve anything too personal. "What's he up to now?"

"He got married about ten years ago," Emily said. "His wife, Sara, and he have three little girls. They're very sweet. Always dressed alike."

"The girls or Steve and his wife?" Greg allowed a smile to twitch at the corners of his lips.

"The girls." She laughed.

"What's he up to? We lost touch when he left for college."

"He's an accountant," she replied. "He's doing pretty well for himself. They live in Billings."

That sounded like Steve. He'd always been the number-crunching sort, acing math classes and taking on the role of class treasurer. Greg would have guessed that he'd end up with a comfortable lifestyle, and Billings was a logical place to land. There had always been something about Steve that Greg hadn't liked, though—a cockiness that rubbed him the wrong way.

Emily poured them each a glass of iced tea, and he took a sip of the sweet brew.

"Did you know Jessica?" she asked.

Greg shook his head. "I think I knew that Steve had

a younger sister, but—" He paused. "No, I didn't know her."

"I'm not sure why she chose me." A blush rose in Emily's cheeks.

"You said you didn't know she was pregnant. Did her brother know?" Greg's gut told him that there was a lot more to this story, but just because a family's story was deep and complicated didn't mean that there was anything criminal going on. Heck, his family had pretty deep and complicated things going on, too.

Emily was silent for a moment, then shrugged. "Not that he said. This is all pretty strange."

He nodded slowly. "So you'd lost touch, and all of a sudden there's a baby in the picture?"

"Pretty much." She let out a sigh. "It feels like a dream right now."

"It'll be an adjustment." He heard the cop-sound in his own voice. It came out naturally, especially when he felt uncomfortable, and this beautiful kindergarten teacher definitely made him uncomfortable.

"So how long have you been in law enforcement?"

"I joined right out of high school. My dad was a cop, too."

"I didn't realize that. I don't think I knew your dad."

"He was before your time." Greg shrugged. The story of his police-chief father wasn't one he intended to tell.

"You've done well for yourself. You're police chief here, you're well respected—"

"Thanks. You've done well, too." He looked around at the rancher.

"Oh, this wasn't on a teacher's salary." She laughed softly. "My grandparents left me an inheritance, and my parents kicked in a graduation gift, which meant I could just afford the mortgage payments."

"You've got family behind you, and that's a good thing."

"Everything is easier with family," she agreed, taking a long sip of iced tea from her glass. "So what about you? Do you have a lot of family around here?"

"Not a lot. We moved out here for my dad's job when I was young, so most of the family is back east."

She nodded thoughtfully, but remained silent.

"Are you doing this alone?" he asked.

A little hiccup-y cry came from the bassinet, and she slid off the stool and went to pick up the baby. Cora wriggled in Emily's arms for a few moments before settling against her neck. Glancing at her watch, Emily walked over to the fridge and grabbed a bottle, his question apparently forgotten.

"I think she's hungry...." Her voice was soft and soothing, her tone different now that the baby was in her arms. After running the bottle under hot water, shaking it up and testing it, she popped the nipple into the baby's mouth, who slurped at it hungrily.

"Yes, I'm doing this alone." Her tone grew quiet as she fed the baby. "I'm single, so this is my chance. I'm not getting any younger, either. I always wanted children of my own, but—" She stopped and laughed self-consciously.

"You must like kids a lot, teaching kindergarten," he said.

"I love kids." She gave him a grin. "Do you?"

"Oh, definitely." He chuckled. "I have a couple of nephews who come to visit me every spring break. We have a great time."

Emily looked down into the infant's face tenderly. She loved the baby already, he could tell. That was a good thing. A very good thing. The image of the crumpled car, the blood and the baby wailing from the backseat was still very fresh in his mind, and seeing her cuddled and loved was helping to dispel it.

"If you ever need anything, just let me know," he said. "And I'm serious about that."

"Thanks." She looked up at him, her dark eyes meeting his warmly.

"The other officers, well…let's just say that Cora stole quite a few hearts, and we all care about her."

Tears misted Emily's eyes at that, and she nodded. "That means a lot. It'll mean a lot to Cora, too."

Cora, who had been busily draining the bottle, slurped the last sip of the milk, and a little white trail dribbled down her chin. Emily lifted the baby onto her shoulder, patting her back gently.

"What about you?" she asked suddenly.

"What about me?" he asked.

"Did you get married? Have a family?"

"No." He shook his head slowly. "Never did."

"Why not?" Emily fixed him with a curious stare, her hand still rhythmically patting Cora's back. She blushed and shook her head. "Sorry, that was blunt." The baby lifted her head and wriggled her legs, then dropped her face back into Emily's neck.

"Why didn't you?" he countered, and she shot him a grin.

"Touché, but I have good reason."

"Oh?" He looked over at her, his interest piqued. "What's your reason?"

She blushed and waved it away with her hand. "It doesn't matter. The fact remains, I'm on my own, but I do have a family behind me, so I'll be all right."

Just then, there was a burp, and Emily looked over at her shoulder, making a face.

"I should have seen that coming," she said with a grimace. There was a nice little patch of baby spit-up on her shoulder, starting to drip. It didn't look comfortable. And he was getting too comfortable. She had a way of making him want to talk, and he knew well enough that he shouldn't be going down this path.

"I should go and let you get cleaned up," he said, pushing himself to his feet.

"I guess so...." She gently laid the baby back into the bassinet and turned her attention back toward him. Despite the soiled shirt, her eyes met his with a cheerful sparkle. "But this was nice."

"It was," he admitted, lulled by that stunning smile of hers.

As Greg made his way back to the front door, he realized something a little disturbing. He'd been looking forward to seeing her and getting this case out of his system, and now he found himself wondering how he might be able to see her again. Instead of closing it, he'd just stuck his foot in the door.

Chapter Three

As Emily pulled up to the little cemetery just outside of town, she could see her extended family already milling about, talking in small groups. She parked her SUV behind her parents' sedan and sat there for a moment. Cora was asleep in her car seat in the back, and Emily looked at the tiny form, her pink tongue sticking out of her mouth. She was adorable, and she'd never remember today—the day her mother was buried. Part of Emily felt guilt for all of this—for not being Jessica, for being the stand-in mother and not the real thing.

Emily smiled wanly as she saw her grandmother tottering past with a cane. Her sixty-year-old son walked along next to her, a hand under her arm. This was what family did. They came together when they needed each other most.

As Emily got out of her vehicle and went around to unfasten Cora's car seat, she noticed her mother walking in her direction. She was a plump woman with red dyed hair, wearing a black-and-white print dress.

"There you are," her mother said as she bustled up. "And there is the little one...."

Her mother's eyes misted, and her chin quivered a little as she looked down at sleeping Cora.

"I'm nervous," Emily admitted quietly.

"Don't be."

"Is it crazy to feel guilty?"

"Yes." Her mother nudged her teasingly, blinking back her tears. "You didn't choose this, sweetheart. Jessica chose you. Feel honored."

Emily nodded and lifted the car seat off the base. It was a lot heavier than just the baby, but she'd always seen mothers packing around car seats with babies inside, so she thought there must be some logic to it. As they walked together over the lush, green grass, Emily looked up at the gray, overcast sky. It was somber and threatening rain, a combination that seemed appropriate today.

"How is Uncle Hank?" Emily scanned the people already there, looking for Jessica's father. His wife had passed away a couple of years ago from breast cancer, and now he'd lost his only daughter.

"He's over there, with Aunt Eunice."

Emily's gaze traveled past one of her cousins with triplet toddlers she was trying to control, to her uncle, who stood a little ways off next to an older woman who was patting his arm. He looked weak and exhausted.

"Poor Uncle Hank...." Emily sighed. She saw him look up and notice her. "He probably wants to see Cora."

They angled their steps in Hank's direction, the soft sod sinking under their heels. The lines of graves were straight and solemn, drawing her gaze along them. All eyes seemed to be on Emily as she passed, but aside from a few waves of greeting, they seemed to sense where she was going and let her continue on her way.

"Isn't that Steve?" Her mother looked across the cemetery. A man was bending down to talk to a little girl. It was her cousin Steve, all right, with his too-serious air that she used to tease him about when they were younger. His wife was slender and petite, and true to form, her navy blue dress matched the three little girls. They seemed to be just arriving, as the toddler was being strapped into a stroller by her father.

Emily was silent for a long moment, watching her cousin. He was a few years older than Emily, a very conservative, straightlaced man with a picture-perfect family. Sara still looked svelte and young, despite three pregnancies, and she had that gentle mother quality about her—the kind of woman you expect could kiss a boo-boo better and halt an escaping toddler in her tracks at the same time. She stood up straight and looked in Emily's direction, but didn't lift a hand in any kind of hello. Emily could feel the tension zipping toward her from all the way across the cemetery.

"Go on and see Uncle Hank," her mother said. "I'll give my condolences to your cousin."

Emily nodded, and her mother gave her arm a quick squeeze before heading off in the other direction on her mission to intercept. A cool breeze picked up, carrying with it the electrical scent of threatening rain, and Emily shivered. She adjusted the knit blanket a little closer around Cora and took a deep breath.

Lord, I can feel the tension already, she prayed silently. *I hate this.*

As she made her way across the sod, an image rose up in her mind of the handsome chief of police. Somehow, the thought of him was comforting, and on a day like this, comfort seemed to be what they all needed. Uncle Hank looked up at Emily morosely as she came up to where he stood. He gave her a small smile of hello and looked down into the car seat. He stretched out a finger to stroke one little hand, then stood up straight again.

"She looks like her mother."

"I thought so, too...." Emily blinked back the tears that misted her eyes. "I thought you might want to see her, Uncle Hank."

"Thanks."

"Why don't you come by later?" Emily asked. "You come hold her anytime you feel like it."

He nodded slowly, then swallowed hard. "I didn't even know..."

"Did anyone?" Emily asked.

"I don't think so. Why didn't she tell us?"

Emily just shook her head. That was the million-dollar question.

"Well, the little one is here, and she'll be much loved." The lines in the older man's face deepened as he looked down into Cora's tiny face. "I wish June could have seen her."

Emily felt her eyes brim with tears at the catch in his voice. "Are you going to be all right, Uncle Hank?"

"Oh—" he took a deep breath "—I'll keep on keeping on, I suppose."

"Cora needs you, too, you know."

He nodded silently. "I still can't believe she didn't tell me. Not even when the baby was born."

The pain he felt was more than loss; it was betrayal. Jessica had been a loved daughter, the girl who looked nothing like either parent, and more like a fairy left by the door. She was slender and beautiful, hair bright red and eyes deepest green. Her mother had often joked that if she hadn't given birth to her herself, she wouldn't have believed that they'd produced her. But the past few years had been hard on the family, and relationships had got strained.

"You were a good dad, Uncle Hank," Emily said softly.

"But was I?" He turned his grief-stricken eyes onto Emily, and she had no answer for him. Emily hadn't seen her cousin in several years, either, a small detail that meant little to a cousin but was heartbreaking for a parent.

"Hi, Dad."

Emily turned to see Steve approaching quickly. He passed Emily without a glance and wrapped his arms around his father's neck. They held each other for a long moment and Emily looked away, sensing their need for some privacy. She stepped back, not wanting to intrude, but as she did so, Steve released his father and looked toward Emily.

"Hi, Em," he said. "Good to see you."

"You, too. I'm sorry about Jessica."

Steve nodded and gave a sad shrug. "This is the baby?"

He bent down over the car seat in Emily's hand and looked at the tiny infant for a long, silent moment.

"Hi," he whispered softly. Cora stirred in her sleep.

"She looks like Jessica, doesn't she?" Emily asked.

Steve looked up at Emily, his expression unreadable. He pushed himself back to his feet and looked up as his wife and daughters approached. Sara came straight toward Emily and bent down to look into the car seat.

"Hi, Cora," she whispered. Sara had perfectly straight, dark hair cut in a short bob. She gave Emily a sad smile. "This must be harder on you, Emily," she said.

Emily wasn't entirely sure what to say.

"A newborn is a big responsibility," Sara went on, her

voice low and sympathetic. "No sleep, the expense, the change in lifestyle…"

"It's all right."

"Well, it is when you have a husband to support you through it all. I can't imagine doing it alone."

"I'm handling it."

"It's been, what, a week?" Sara smiled wanly. "Trust me. I've done this three times. This is the easy part."

With a smooth smile, Sara turned her attention to her father-in-law, putting her arms around him and crooning out her condolences. Emily took a deep breath. What were her responsibilities here?

"I'm just going to say hello to…" Emily started to edge away from the group, not even bothering to finish her sentence.

"Wait, Em." It was Steve. He walked toward her, shoving his hands into his pockets. "Can we talk?"

"Sure." Emily waited till he was at her side, then started walking back toward the rest of the family. Steve matched her pace.

"This can't be easy for you."

"That's what Sara said."

"Oh, come on, Em. You're single. Do you ever want to get married? Finding a guy with a baby isn't going to be easy."

"Don't worry yourself over my romantic life," she retorted. "Look, Steve, I know this is really hard. None of us knew about this baby. Jessica is gone. It's a hard time on the whole family."

"No, it's worse for me."

"Of course. Jessica was your sister. I didn't mean to imply—"

"And Cora is my niece. She's only your—what— second cousin?"

The scent of the approaching rain was getting stronger now, and the wind started to pick up. She shivered and began to walk faster.

"What do you want, Steve?"

"She belongs with me and Sara."

"What do you mean?"

"We're her closest relatives. You aren't."

"Jessica chose me. This wasn't my idea. She named me Cora's guardian in her will."

Steve stopped, and Emily turned to face him. She could hear the low rumble of thunder far off in the distance and tears welled up in her eyes. What did he want from her? Did he expect her to just hand the baby over and walk away?

"You don't want this." Steve shook his head slowly, as if disappointed with a small child. "It might seem all romantic and sweet now, but babies are a huge amount of work. What about your career?"

"Let me worry about that, Steve. I'm a grown woman."

"Fine. But when you change your mind, call me. I'll come and get her."

The dripping condescension in his voice was almost more than Emily could bear, and she turned around and walked away, moving toward the grave site. The service would begin soon, and they would all pay their last respects to Jessica Shaw.

When Emily looked back, she saw Sara staring after her with a strange intensity, the wind ruffling her short hair and her little girls standing at her knees. Uncle Hank didn't seem to be noticing very much in his grief, and he was talking to Emily's father, both men nodding sadly.

They expected to bring Cora home with them today, she realized with a chill. Did Steve and Sara really think it would be that easy, to simply point out the hard work a baby would be and have her pass Cora off like a piece of luggage? That image of Chief Greg Taylor rose in her mind again, and she knew exactly who she needed to talk to—the one person without a personal interest in this.

"The service is going to start soon." Emily looked up in relief to see the compassionate face of her mother. "Come on, sweetie."

Together, they made their way with the rest of the family toward the grave site where the minister was waiting, the pages of his Bible fluttering in the rising wind. It was time to say their goodbyes.

Rain pelted the sidewalk outside Greg's office window. The afternoon light turned almost dusky in the rainstorm, and he leaned his elbows on his desk and looked out at the downpour. The plains offered little shelter from a summer storm, and as the clouds gathered, the wind whistled through the buildings. The air smelled of electricity and wet earth, and he inhaled deeply, enjoying the finger of air that wriggled through the crack of the open window. It was an old building, the kind with windows that opened at the top, leaning back on a brass hinge, and today he was thankful for the connection to the outdoors.

It had been a long morning. Before coming into work, he'd dropped by the nursing home to see his mother. The dementia was worse lately. A few months ago she remembered him perfectly and would look up at him with a smile, but this morning she frowned at him in confusion.

"Why are the police here?" she asked. "Is everyone all right?"

He hated scaring her like that.

"Yes, ma'am," he'd said softly. "Everything is fine. I'm sorry to disturb you."

He knew better than to try to remind her of who he was. It would only upset her further—she would seem to remember for a moment, and then suddenly look fearful, wondering why an officer was in her room and what the bad news must be. She always associated police with bad news when she was confused.

One of the nurses had given him a sympathetic pat on the arm, promising to call him when she was more aware.

What he hated worse than scaring his own mother was the helplessness. As a cop, he was used to solving problems. He had the authority to stop bad things from happening, and he made sure he did that. He was a big man, muscular and tall, and he was accustomed to the automatic respect his physique demanded, but when it came to his mother, none of these things mattered. She didn't see him as her protector; she saw him as a threat. He wanted to do something—fix it, if he could. He wanted to put his big, brawny body between his mother and the disease that snipped away at her memories, but he couldn't.

Sitting at his desk, he'd been going through the mounds of paperwork that came with his position, but his mind kept slipping back to his mother. After his dad was gone, his mother had a lot more to worry about, raising two kids on her own. She went back to work as a secretary. It was a job she was good at, but it kept her away from home more often than she liked.

Greg and his sister, Lynn, generally looked out for each other after school. But during school hours, Richard Pike, one of the bigger guys in his class, decided it was his life's mission to make Greg as miserable as possible. From his head being plunged into the toilet to being beaten up during recess, Greg's school life had been misery. Then he'd come home to the empty house and he'd sit there watching whatever show was on, trying to forget about the ache in his heart from losing his dad, and trying not to think about the next day, when he'd have to go back to school and face Richard all over again. Times like those, all he wanted was a hug from his mom, but she wouldn't be home from work for hours yet.

That was before he learned how to box.

His mother wasn't the only person on his mind, however. Thoughts of Emily had been worming their way in there, too…images of her with Cora in her arms and that sparkle in her eye just before a smile slid onto her face. Greg knew all too well that mixing work with pleasure was a really bad idea, but somehow his thoughts of Emily were the most comfortable thoughts available to him, so he didn't push them away.

Scanning a form and signing the bottom, he put the paper aside and flipped down to the next triplicate form waiting for his attention. Outside, thunder boomed and the room suddenly lit up with a flash of lightning. He glanced up again. The wind had shifted direction, blowing rain in through the open window, and he stood up to shut it.

There was a tap on the door, and as he flicked the lock on the window into place, his secretary, Joyce, poked her head in.

"Chief? There's a Miss Shaw to see you. Do you have time?"

"Yes, definitely."

He'd answered rather quickly, to his chagrin, and Joyce smothered a smile. He hated it when she thought she could read him like a book, and he gave her an annoyed look as she stepped back and pushed the door open.

"Come on in, Miss Shaw," she said, and she gave Greg one more look of amused knowing. Emily stepped inside, Cora's car seat in one hand, a blanket draped over it. Emily, on the other hand, was completely drenched. Her hair was slicked down against her head, and a trickle of water ran down her cheek. She wore a black pantsuit that was equally sodden.

"What happened to you?" he asked, coming toward her. "Joyce, would you go get some towels, please?"

"You bet, Chief."

Emily shrugged and laughed self-consciously. "It was really coming down out there. I should have just waited in my car till it let up, but then I thought I could make it and—" she waved her hand "—it doesn't matter."

Greg laughed. "Well, it's nice to see you. Cora looks dry."

Emily looked down at Cora with a tender smile. "Warm and dry," she agreed.

"Here." Greg helped her to peel off the black suit jacket she wore, and he took his sport coat off the hanger on the back of his door. Draping it over her shoulders, she shivered involuntarily and looked up at him gratefully. "Have a seat."

Emily sank into the chair across from his desk. He could see the tension in her face, along her jaw and around her eyes.

"I hope I'm not disturbing you."

"It's a welcome break." He gestured to the pile of paperwork. "So how are you?"

"I'm fine." She gave him a smile that didn't reach her eyes, then she shrugged. "I'm not fine. Today was Jessica's funeral."

"That's right. I'm sorry I wasn't there." He avoided the funerals. It was part of his attempt to compartmentalize the suffering he had to see in this line of work.

"No, it's all right. Don't worry about that." She shook her head, dismissing it. "Steve was there."

"Oh, how is he?"

"Steve is Steve." She gave him a tight smile. "He wants me to give him custody of Cora."

"I see." Greg wasn't entirely surprised to hear this. Custody was a complicated thing at the best of times, but it got worse when the children were so tiny. Everyone wanted to raise a baby. It was the kids who were old enough to have attitude and emotional issues that got shuffled around a lot.

"He was pretty pushy about it. Sara was… I don't know how to describe her. She was pretty intense. I got the distinct impression that they expected me to hand Cora over, and they'd go home with her today."

"Did they say that?"

"Not exactly." Emily sighed and looked away for a moment. "I know I probably sound like a crazy person right now, but they kind of scared me."

"No, you don't sound crazy."

"Thanks." She gave him a grateful smile. "I just wanted to come by and pick your brain a little."

"My pleasure." He leaned back in his chair, and just then, the door opened again, and Joyce came in with a couple of towels from the women's locker room.

"Thank you," Emily said, taking one and shaking it out. She blotted her face and hair. Joyce slipped back out without a word.

Emily peeked down under the blanket at the sleeping baby and then let the towel fall to her lap. She looked at Greg silently for a long moment, worry creasing her brow. He let the silence stretch, waiting for her to speak.

"Greg, what happens in these cases?" she asked finally.

"You're the guardian named in the will," he said. "That makes you her legal guardian, and Steve can't just bully you into changing that."

She nodded. "Is that final?"

"Well…" He didn't want to scare her, but he didn't want to lie to her, either. "Nothing is ever entirely final, I suppose. Unless you adopt her."

"Can Steve contest the will?" she asked.

"In theory. Do you think he'd go that far?"

Emily sighed. "I have no idea, but he was pretty focused on convincing me to give her up today at the funeral."

A finger of irritation wormed through his stomach. He didn't like the thought of someone trying to bully her, and it made him want to throw his weight around a little. Instead of voicing his feelings, he asked, "Did he threaten you?"

"No." She laughed softly. "This is Steve we're talking about. He got snide and condescending, but that was it. He's my cousin, after all."

Greg made a noncommittal sound. Yes, he remembered Steve well. He'd been both snide and condescending in high school, too. He'd never been cruel on the level of Richard Pike, but he'd made a couple of junior guys pretty miserable senior year, and Greg had taken it upon himself to stand up for them. Steve was a bully, and if there was one thing Greg could not abide, it was a bully.

"Do you want to raise Cora?" Greg asked, changing the subject.

"More than anything. I know this seems strange because I'm not exactly in a position to be taking children into my home, but I do. I've fallen in love with her. I don't want to give her up."

He nodded silently. Of course she didn't. Who wouldn't fall in love with that baby? The entire department here in Haggerston had fallen in love with her.

"Have you seen these sorts of cases before?" she asked, her full attention focused on his face.

He nodded slowly. "Yes, a few times."

"What normally happens?"

"Well, normally, the parents have named the godparents in their will and nothing changes."

She nodded, visibly relaxing. "Have you ever seen a will contested?"

Greg sighed. "It's probably best not to worry about this sort of thing unless you have to."

"Maybe so, but I'm worried now." She didn't look the least bit daunted. "What happens when the will gets contested?"

"It gets ugly," he admitted. "Everyone loves the baby and wants to raise it. Everyone has a reason why the other people are a terrible choice. People say things they can't take back and close-knit, loving families end up fractured. It can get really bad."

"That's what I was afraid of." Her voice softened, and he had to lean forward with a creak of his chair to catch her words.

"That doesn't mean that will happen to you," he added. "You're her legal guardian, okay? That hasn't been contested."

She nodded. "I know. Thanks." She slipped his jacket off her shoulders and rose to her feet. "I appreciate this."

Greg stood up, too, and he came around his desk, then

sat on the edge of it. "I'm not a father," he said. "But I deal with a lot of parents in this job."

"Me, too." She chuckled.

"Yeah, that's true." He shot her a grin. "Then you've probably been told the same things I've been told. Parents start worrying from birth. They worry about all sorts of worst-case scenarios, most of which never happen."

"So don't be silly?" she asked.

"Not at all." He chuckled. "I was going to say that worrying is part of the package when you're a parent. Maybe just realize that you're not alone in your worries. Consider it more a welcome to the club."

Emily's warm gaze met his, and her eyes crinkled up into a smile. "That's the sweetest thing I've heard all day."

Greg felt a sudden wave of satisfaction. "Anytime." He meant it more than she realized, he was sure.

Just then, Cora began to fuss, and Emily rocked the car seat gently. "I'd better get her home," she said quietly. "I don't have another bottle with me."

"Take care."

Emily turned toward the door and opened it.

"Oh, and Emily—"

She turned back, those deep brown eyes meeting his once more.

"Come by anytime, okay? I mean that."

"Thanks." She flashed him a smile. "I appreciate it."

With that, she slipped out, and he listened to the sound of her heels clicking as she made her way through the station, the rhythm blending into the hustle and bustle of police activity. With a smile to himself, he turned back to his paperwork.

Chapter Four

A couple of days later, on a warm summer evening, Emily sat on the couch across from her two friends, Nina and Beth. Beth sat with her legs tucked up underneath her, her pregnant belly protruding out in front of her. She was only about six months along, but she was all tummy, as she put it. She had a mop of curly mouse-brown hair and two swollen bare feet that were normally swathed in Birkenstocks. She rubbed her stomach absently, looking over at Cora, who lay nestled in Nina's arms.

Nina sat next to Beth, looking down at the tiny infant with a wistful look on her face. Her blond hair was cut short in a pixie cut, and her makeup was impeccable. With legs a mile long, Nina had pretty much everything that Emily envied.

"She's beautiful." Beth looked over at Emily and shook her head in wonder. "I can't believe that you have a baby."

"Me, neither." Emily grinned over at her. "You're not far behind, you know."

"Three months." Beth leaned her head back against the couch. "I'm going to be the size of a house!"

"But a cute house." Nina shot Beth a teasing look.

"Oh, stop worrying. You'll be fine. You're blissfully married to Howard. He'll love you, anyway."

Emily looked over at her two best friends. They'd been there for each other since their idealistic days when Beth was a feminist with a loudspeaker, and Nina was plotting her financial empire. Emily had been the boring one—taking early childhood education and going to bed at sensible hours. In the meantime, life had unfurled in that way it always seemed to, in the very last way any of them expected.

Nina looked up with a glint in her eye. "What about this Chief Taylor, Em?"

"What about him?" Emily pasted on her most innocent look.

"Well, you've dropped his name often enough," Beth pointed out.

"There's nothing to tell." Emily shrugged. "He was the one who dropped Cora off, so it stands to reason that we'd talk from time to time."

Nina and Beth exchanged a look.

"Actually, it doesn't stand to reason at all," Nina quipped with a grin.

"He knew my cousin, so we're acquainted with some of the same people." There was no use trying to explain this to Nina and Beth when they had that look on their faces. She laughed and shook her head.

"So what's he like?" Beth asked.

"Nice," Emily said.

"Cute?" Nina prodded.

"Yeah, he's a good-looking guy." Emily tried to keep her tone neutral.

"Huh." Beth nodded. "And you manage to keep conversation going between the two of you."

"Oh, stop it." Emily laughed. "He's the chief of police

and nothing more. In fact, if anything, he seems really uncomfortable and serious around me. So don't be getting your hopes up."

"You sure?" Nina pressed. "We're a little worried about how long you've stayed single."

"Look who's talking!" Emily laughed.

"This baby needs a change." Nina lifted Cora out of her lap and deposited her with Emily. Just then, the phone rang.

"Would you mind getting that?" Emily asked.

Beth leaned over to grab the handset and picked it up. "Hello?"

Cora kicked her legs happily as Emily set to work on the diaper.

"Just a minute." Beth pushed herself out of her seat and brought the phone to Emily.

"A lawyer?" she whispered, passing the handset over.

Emily felt her heart speed up as she took the phone from her friend's hand. Beth took over with Cora as Emily answered the phone.

"This is Emily Shaw."

"Hello, Miss Shaw, this is Paul Hanson."

"Mr. Hanson. How are you?" It was her lawyer who had been dealing with the paperwork for her guardianship.

"I'm sorry to call so late, but I thought you'd want to know."

"What's going on?" Emily's voice sounded breathless in her own ears.

"Someone is contesting your guardianship." His voice was quiet and professional. "A Mr. Steven Shaw."

"My cousin…"

"He's filed the paperwork."

"What does this mean?"

"That's up to you, really," he replied. "Do you want to fight this?"

Emily looked over at her friends, sadness welling up inside of her. "I'd better give you a call back," she said, trying to control the tremor in her voice. "Thanks for letting me know."

"Absolutely. Call me tomorrow morning, if you can, so I know how you want to proceed."

"Thank you."

As she hung up the phone, Beth and Nina looked at her mutely, their eyes betraying their apprehension.

"Well…" Emily said, the tears welling up in her eyes. "Steve is contesting my right to raise Cora."

"Oh, Em," Beth breathed.

Oh, God, is this it? Is this my brush with motherhood?

"What will you do?" Nina asked.

Beth just stood there, a hand protectively over her belly and tears misting her eyes. "Let's pray."

They didn't pray together often. It wasn't their style; but tonight it felt right. Standing there with her two best friends, the three women bowed their heads.

Nate's Steak was a local joint that had been thriving for the past thirty-five years, Nate retired and left the place to his son, Mike, who didn't change a thing. The wings came in three flavors: hot, really hot and honey garlic, and the steaks were grilled to perfection. There was a reason why the officers at Haggerston made this their favorite meet-up place.

The sun was setting over the town when Greg parked in front of Nate's Steak and stepped out into the warm evening air. The smell of grilling meat met the sweet scent of hydrangeas that hung in baskets along the downtown streets. Greg looked around the parking lot and

spotted three cruisers and a few pickup trucks he recognized from some nearby ranches. He'd be in good
company tonight.

As Greg stepped inside, he was met with the hum of
voices, the clink of knives and forks against dishes and
the general hubbub from the kitchen. Scanning the few
tables, he nodded to the people he knew, then headed
toward the back of the restaurant where the other officers were.

"Hi, Chief," Benny called, and the others looked up
in welcome.

"Hi." Greg pulled up a chair. "What's good tonight?"

"Does it matter?" Nancy asked with a laugh. She was
a muscular officer with a steady gaze and a gorgeous
smile. Her hair was pulled back in a low-maintenance
ponytail, but she was out of uniform, sporting jeans and
a T-shirt from Graceland.

"You want the regular, Chief?" Mike called from the
counter. Greg gave a thumbs-up and Mike disappeared
into the kitchen. He ordered the same thing every time
he came by: hot wings and an herbal tea.

"Couldn't get enough of us, Nancy?" Greg joked.

"Just can't stay away." Her tone was dry. "Actually,
this beat grocery shopping."

"And reruns on TV," Benny added. Nancy gave a
shrug of agreement. A jukebox started playing a honky-
tonk tune, and Benny tapped the table in time to the
music.

"How about you, Chief?" Nancy asked. "Long day?"

Greg nodded, then frowned. "Actually, I've been
thinking about that 11-80 the other day—the one with
the baby."

"How's Sweet pea doing?" Benny asked with a grin.
They'd nicknamed her Sweet pea that night when Greg

brought her back to the station, and Benny had settled in with a bottle of formula and held her for a solid hour.

"She's doing great." Greg could feel the smile coming to his face. "She is very well cared for."

Emily Shaw had been on his mind more often than he cared to admit, but his concern for the case was more than the beautiful kindergarten teacher with her quick smile.

"So what's not sitting right with you, Chief?" Nancy leaned forward.

"What did we find in the victim's car?" Greg asked. "The accident happened outside of Haggerston, so we're assuming she was on her way here. She had family here, after all."

"That's right." Benny nodded. "Emily Shaw, for one."

Greg nodded. Emily topped his list, too, especially since Jessica Shaw had thought enough of her to name her godmother, but even Emily seemed surprised by the honor. Something felt wrong.

"But what did she have with her? A diaper bag and a purse with a toothbrush inside. She was two hours from Billings, where she lived. Does that seem right?"

"Two hours there and another two back..." Benny shrugged. "Could have been a day trip."

"What do you think, Nancy?"

"As a woman?"

"Yes, as a woman."

Nancy gave him a smug look. "So now I'm a woman, am I? I'm just one of the guys when I beat you at push-ups."

Greg shook his head and laughed. "Don't rub it in. What do you think?"

"No woman travels two hours one way with a newborn and only brings a toothbrush and a diaper bag. No extra clothes for the baby or anything." Nancy shrugged. "Something feels off with that."

"Who does that?" Greg asked.

"A distressed woman," Nancy replied. "That packing didn't show any forethought. She was upset about something."

Greg nodded. "That's what I was thinking, too."

"Or a woman who might not make great decisions at the best of times," Benny said.

Greg gave a smile of thanks to the server as his wings and tea arrived. The wings were plump and saucy, and the little dish of blue cheese dressing on the side was overflowing onto the wings. Crunching on a carrot stick, he looked across the table at Benny and Nancy thoughtfully.

"So was she running away from something?"

"Or someone?" Benny took a sip of his cola and shrugged.

Greg shook his head and picked up a wing. "Wish it made more sense."

"Is the family suspicious?" Benny inquired.

Greg shook his head. "Not that anyone has mentioned, formally or otherwise."

He sank his teeth into one of the wings, the spicy sauce making his mouth water. For a few minutes he put his attention into his food, and when he'd sucked the third bone clean, Nancy suddenly said, "If the victim thought someone had tried to kill her, she would have mentioned it, don't you think? She was alert."

"But in shock," Benny pointed out.

Nancy nodded and gave a shrug. "Something isn't adding up."

"It might be nothing criminal at all," Greg agreed, "but something is nagging at me with this case."

"*Is* it a case right now, Chief?" Benny asked.

"I'm not saying that I think this was murder." Greg frowned thoughtfully. "I'm going to need a little more information, though, before I formally close the case."

Chapter Five

The next evening, Emily pulled open McRuben's front door, a blast of air-conditioning meeting her in a welcoming wave. There was no lineup, and the only other patron was an old man nursing a coffee in a disposable cup by the bathrooms.

A bored teenager took her order, and Emily watched in silent delight as he filled her fries up to overflowing. When the boxed burger was deposited onto her plastic tray, Emily's mouth watered in anticipation. Extra pickles, extra mayo and a dab of their secret sauce... This was the kind of dinner she looked forward to more than she cared to admit.

"Need a hand with that?"

Emily started at the familiar voice and looked up to see Chief Taylor standing there in uniform.

"Chief!" She looked down at her tray piled high with burger, fries, a milk shake and a sundae and felt her cheeks heat.

"Get me the same, would you?" He pointed to her tray and put a bill on the counter.

"Do you have a secret love of fast food?" she teased.

"I'm actually here for a perfectly professional excuse." He shot her a grin, the most relaxed Emily had seen him yet.

"I don't believe you." She felt a smile tickle the corners of her mouth.

"All right, truth be told, I want a burger. But since you're here, it could save me some time."

"That's more like it." She chuckled, picking up Cora's car seat.

"Let me carry this for you." He picked up her tray.

Leading the way to a booth by a window, Emily looked back over her shoulder. "So what is this good professional excuse of yours?"

"Just some unanswered questions, mostly, Miss Shaw."

Greg waited until Emily had Cora settled on the bench beside her before he eased into the seat opposite her.

He nodded his thanks to the teen who put down an identical tray to Emily's in front of him. "About Jessica—does anyone know why she was coming to Haggerston?"

Emily shook her head. "I don't know, but I guess I'd assumed she'd been on her way here. Her dad was here, after all. I did ask people at the funeral, but no one was really sure."

He unwrapped the burger and peeked inside, his expression unreadable. "What is this?"

Emily laughed. "You did ask for what I was having…. It's a burger with extra pickles, mayo and secret sauce. It's delicious. Don't knock it till you've tried it."

Greg took a cautious bite, then smiled. "Good." He wiped the corners of his mouth with a napkin. "I normally do extra bacon and tomato."

Emily raised her eyebrows as an idea struck her. "I

should start putting some bacon on this. That would be perfect."

Greg shot her an amused look and then sobered. "So no one knew Jessica was coming?"

Emily shook her head. "Everyone was saying the same thing—we had no idea she was pregnant, let alone already a mother. We hadn't heard from her in a long time."

Greg nodded slowly. "Did she have drug problems? What would isolate her from her family like that?"

"Well…" Emily opened a ketchup package and made a little mound to dip her fries into. "Her parents were good Christian people, and Jessica was the black sheep of the family. She was the one who went out partying as a teenager and defied her parents at every turn." She shrugged. "When she moved out of her parents' house and went off to the city, she came back a couple of times for family events, but things were pretty strained between her and her parents."

"But no substance-abuse problems?"

Emily shook her head, opening another packet of ketchup as she talked. "I think their biggest problem was that she was sleeping around, and they didn't like it. She drank a little at parties, but I don't think she was ever involved in drugs."

"Why not?"

"She put herself through a fine-arts degree," Emily said, raising her gaze to meet his. "She painted and drew. She was quite the artist. She worked too hard to get that degree on her own. She couldn't have done it high."

"So more of a free spirit."

Emily nodded. "Don't you remember her from Steve?"

"No." He shook his head and popped a fry into his

mouth. "I didn't know Steve terribly well, not well enough to know his sister."

"Why does any of this matter?" she asked, turning her attention to the food in front of her. She took a bite of her burger, the mixture of meat and condiments hitting her brain right in the pleasure center. Greg looked at her thoughtfully for a long moment, as if weighing his words. Finally, he shrugged.

"Maybe it doesn't," he admitted. "I just don't feel quite right about all of this. There's something missing. It might be nothing, but…" He shrugged again.

Emily licked a dab of ketchup off her finger, regarding Greg thoughtfully. Tiny lines were starting to appear around his eyes, and she could see that he shouldered a great deal of stress. He had the rugged features of a man accustomed to hiding his thoughts, but she could see something behind his eyes that she recognized—kindness.

"I suppose I should tell you," Emily said quietly, "that Steve is contesting my custody of the baby."

Greg winced, then nodded. "Yeah, I could see that coming."

Emily shot him a quizzical look, and he put his hands up. "Not because you aren't an excellent choice to raise the baby, but because these things do tend to happen."

Emily sighed. "Well, regardless, I have a big decision to make."

"What decision is that?"

"Whether to fight this in court or not."

"That is a big decision." He gave her a sympathetic look. "I'm sorry."

"It's okay." She smiled sadly. "I just don't know what the best thing is for Cora. A big legal battle hardly seems in her best interest, but then, Jessica chose me, and I'd like to think that was for a reason."

Greg sighed. "So how are you holding up?"

"I have good friends, but the family is already choosing sides. My mom will always be behind me, but I was close to my uncle Hank, too—that's Jessica's dad. He'll want his son to raise Cora, no doubt…"

"It's getting complicated," he said softly.

"Very."

"What do you want?" he asked.

"To raise this baby." She looked over at Cora sleeping peacefully in the car seat. "I can't have children of my own."

"Oh, I see." He nodded and took a bite of his burger.

Stupid, she thought to herself. It was a personal thing to blurt out, and she wished she could take the words back. What did Greg want to know about her fertility? *Seriously, Emily,* she chastised herself.

"So what are you going to do?" he asked.

"I don't know." She took a long, creamy sip of her milk shake. "It's just so complicated."

"I can see that." His blue eyes met hers, and she was relieved to see compassion in them.

"I wish I knew why Jessica chose me instead of her brother. If I knew that, I'd know if I should be fighting for this or not. I need to know what she wanted, really wanted."

He nodded slowly and leaned back in his chair. The comfortable quiet stretched out between them as they each finished their burgers.

"Greg?"

He raised his eyebrows in response.

"Are you going to be investigating my cousin's death?"

"I'll be looking into it," he said. "I don't have any reason to suspect foul play, but I'd like to get a few questions answered to put my own mind at ease."

"While you're doing that, would you mind keeping an eye open for something that might explain why she chose me?" Emily asked.

"Like what?"

"I wish I knew. I just need a few answers, too, about now, and I don't know how to get them."

Greg was silent for a moment, his gaze moving slowly over her face. His blue eyes seemed to be filled with conflicting emotions, something he wasn't hiding very well. Finally, he took a deep breath. "Sure."

"Really?" Emily laughed nervously. "I didn't think you'd agree."

Greg smiled at that. "I think you could use a favor about now."

"Thank you. This means a lot to me."

Just then, Cora began to cry, a thin, hiccup-y wail coming from the car seat, and Emily rummaged through the baby bag for a bottle.

"I'm prepared." She gave him a wink and gently picked up the wriggling Cora in her arms.

Emily tried to give Cora the bottle, but the baby scrunched her eyes shut and wailed all the louder, turning her face away from the milk. Emily patted her and shushed her, but to no avail. She peeked in the diaper and felt her little face for fever. At first, Greg's thoughts were focused on the crying, wondering when it would stop, but then he saw Emily's face and he felt a sudden surge of sympathy. She looked ready to cry, too.

"What's the matter?" Greg asked.

Tears welled up in Emily's eyes, and she shook her head. "I'm not her mother."

Greg could hear the pain in Emily's voice as she said it, and the thought of the tiny thing crying desperately to find her mother—the mother who had been absent for a couple of weeks now—was heartrending.

Cora wailed harder, her face turning red as she cried out her frustration or grief, Emily patting her little rump and shushing fruitlessly. The restaurant was empty except for them, and when he looked over at the teens working, he found them staring.

"Can I try?" he suddenly asked, and as the words came out of his mouth, he was already regretting them. He was more of an iron-pumping kind of guy than a baby-soothing kind of guy, but there was something about the sadness in Emily and the unwanted audience that made him want to fix it if he could.

Emily agreed mutely, and he took the squirming infant out of her arms. What was he thinking? Cora screamed, her eyes squished shut and her tiny tongue quivering with the effort of her wails. When he tried to hold her close, she writhed and wriggled. He wasn't sure exactly how to hold her, but he decided to simply use logic. When apprehending a suspect, first you needed to stop the perpetrator and then subdue the limbs. Cora's legs were squirming quite actively, so he simply pushed the little knees up and pulled her against his chest. Once she was there, she seemed a bit surprised by her position, so he took advantage of the pause in her cries to hum a low, soft note.

It wasn't a song. It wasn't anything, really, just a low sound in his throat that rumbled in his chest. Cora gave a few more squirms, then leaned her tired little head onto his chest, listening to the sound. Emily came around to his side of the table.

"Have some milk, sweetie," Emily murmured, and she slid the bottle's nipple into Cora's mouth. The infant started to suck noisily.

"There." Greg caught her eye and grinned. "Now don't move…"

Emily gave him an impressed look. "Wow, you're good with babies."

"I'm normally not."

"How did you know what to do?"

"Lucky guess?" He looked down at the top of Cora's little head with the damp little swirls of golden-red hair. "I think I just surprised her."

The sound of Cora's soft slurps as she drank her milk filled the space between them, and he looked down at Emily with her dark hair swept away from her face and her long lashes brushing her cheeks with each blink. She sat close to him on the bench as she held the bottle for the baby to drink, and the soft scent of her shampoo mingled with the scent of baby. Just another couple of inches and she could rest her head on his shoulder, too. He pulled his thoughts away from dangerous ground.

"I'll have to remember that trick." She smiled sadly. "I can't change the fact that I'm not her mom."

"Steve's wife wouldn't be her biological mother, either."

"Well, that's true." Some of the sadness left her eyes, and he felt gratified to see it. She was hard on herself, that much was obvious. And she was under a tremendous amount of pressure.

What would it be like to belong with Emily and Cora? This was a sweet moment with the baby in his arms, drinking her bottle, and Emily so close to him that if he just leaned over... No, this wasn't productive. There was no point in imagining what it would be like to have a family—to have them.

"Maybe you should take her back," Greg said gruffly.

"Oh, no," Emily replied, nonplussed. "You seem fine, and she seems happy."

With that, Cora finished the bottle and Emily moved around to her seat across the table from him. Greg looked from Emily to Cora and back to Emily again.

"Burp her, would you?" Emily said. "Here's a cloth."

She said it so matter-of-factly, as if asking someone to burp a baby was the most natural thing in the world, that he found himself wondering if it weren't in fact the most natural thing in the world. He took the proffered cloth and put it over his shoulder the way he'd seen Emily do it. Granted, she was more graceful, but after a couple of tries he managed it, and he started to gently tap Cora's back.

"You know, I used to see myself with a whole houseful of kids." Emily turned her attention to her fries, swirling them slowly through the ketchup. "I don't even know why I thought I'd have so many. I suppose it comes with always having a class full of five-year-olds."

"And now?"

"Now I'm grateful for the chance to raise one child. It's all in perspective."

Cora let out a resounding burp, and Greg looked down at her with a grin. He'd never expected burping a baby to be so...satisfying. It was as if he'd just slam-dunked.

"Nicely done." Emily grinned at him, popping another fry in her mouth. "What about you? Do you ever think about having kids?"

Greg felt the moment disintegrating around him, caving in on itself like the old mall when a wrecking ball connected with a load-bearing wall. He shook his head.

"Not at all?" Her brow furrowed as her eyes met his. "You don't want kids?"

"No," he said. "I don't."

It was the truth, wasn't it? He couldn't lie to her, but he could see the disappointment in her eyes as he admitted what was inside of him. No matter how adorable Cora was, no matter how sweet it might feel to imagine having a family of his own, children were simply out of the question.

Chapter Six

The next day, Emily stood at the kitchen sink washing a sink load of dishes while her mother rocked Cora. The sink was loaded full of pots and pans, some muffin tins sitting to the side taunting her with the sheer amount of scrubbing they were going to require. It was a bright and sunny day, and as Emily stood there by the sink, wrist-deep in soapy water, she could see some robins poking through her lawn in the shade of an apple tree. It was peaceful.

Emily's mother stood behind her, Cora in her arms. She looked down at the baby with the wide-eyed expression people used with babies, and Cora looked entranced. Emily chuckled softly as she rinsed another mug and put it in the dish rack.

"Uncle Hank came by this morning," Emily said.

"Poor man." Her mother sighed. "Did seeing Cora help him at all?"

"I don't know." Emily put her attention into some egg welded onto a plate. "He didn't stay long. He cuddled her for a little while, then he said he had to go."

"I can't imagine how he must be feeling right now...." Her mother put Cora up onto her shoulder and leaned against the island. "To lose a daughter." She shook her head. "It's unthinkable."

Emily nodded.

"He and Jessica had a complicated relationship," her mother commented thoughtfully. "That would almost make it worse, I think."

"What happened between them?"

"He thought that being tough on Jessica would straighten her out." Her mother shrugged her shoulders. "Was he wrong? I guess so, considering that she left and never really came back. He thought she needed more discipline, and by the time he realized he was wrong in that call, it was too late."

Emily pulled another plate out of the sudsy water and looked back at her mother. "I think it did him some good. He said Cora looks a lot like Jessica did as a baby."

"She does, doesn't she?" The older woman looked down at Cora's little face. Her mother had been a natural redhead once upon a time, and now she dyed it back to red, but it never looked very natural anymore. The line of white at her roots didn't help.

Emily was avoiding the topic that was on her mind, but she was afraid to bring it up. Had Uncle Hank felt uncomfortable in her home because of Steve contesting custody? Did he think she was taking something away from his family? She washed a pot, rinsing it in hot water and listening to the sound of her mother making mouth noises for Cora.

"What about the custody thing?" Emily asked finally.

"What do you mean?" her mother asked.

"Has anyone said anything?"

Her mother was silent for a long moment. Then she took a deep breath. "Uncle Hank hasn't said anything, but he isn't much of a talker. Your aunts didn't think too much of Jessica, so they think that she should have left her daughter to Steven. He was her brother, after all. Grandma is just really sad. She says that Jessica did a good thing by leaving Cora to you, and she thinks Steven is being willfully difficult...."

Emily listened as her mother went on with a description of everyone's opinions on the matter. She knew that every family member would have one, but it was another thing hearing them all. She probably shouldn't have asked.

"...Aunt Helen thinks that Sara wants to raise Cora because she gave Jessica such a hard time when they first got married. She thought Jessica was far beneath her and didn't make any bones about it. Aunt Helen thinks that Sara feels like she needs to prove something. My cousin, Edith, on the other hand..."

"Mom?"

Her mother stopped. "Yes, dear?"

"What about you?"

"I think that Jessica made the best choice in choosing you. I think Cora would be a lucky girl to grow up with a kind and loving mother like you."

Emily shot her mother a grateful smile. "I love you, Mom."

"I love you, too, sweetie." Her mother smiled. "So what are you going to do?"

"I'm not entirely sure. What would happen if I fought this?"

"It's hard to tell." Her mother laid Cora back in the bassinet and dangled a toy above her. "Steven would be angry, very angry. It would really affect your relationship with him."

"And Uncle Hank?"

"He's just grieving Jessica right now. I don't know. People would choose sides…."

That was exactly what Emily was afraid of—a big, tragic divide in a large family. The Shaws had big yearly family picnics. Everyone came with all of their children and grandchildren. There were games, more burgers than anyone could eat and a whole lot of gossip and chatter. Emily met cousins she saw only once a year, but it felt good to be a part of the Shaw clan. They had something special—a unity that defied the modern tendency to fracture.

"And what if I lost this case?" That was Emily's biggest fear—that after all of this trauma to the family, she'd lose the case anyhow and have nothing to show for it.

Her mother didn't answer that. She just exchanged a sad look with her daughter.

"Is it worth it?" Emily asked.

"Only you can answer that."

That was true enough, and Emily knew it. It was almost harder that way—having to make this decision that would affect all of them on her own. Jessica had named her the guardian of her daughter. Emily was the one with legal rights to the baby, and she was the one being brought into court about it. No one else could make this decision for her.

"I think this is different for you because of your condition." Her mother sighed. "You have more to lose."

Emily couldn't help but agree. It had been two years since her doctor explained her medical situation to her. There had been months of testing, culminating in a day of exploratory surgery. When she awoke from the anesthetic, her doctor sat down beside her bed and met her gaze levelly.

"It's worse than we thought, Emily."

"How bad is it?"

"The endometriosis has affected every part of your reproductive system. This is a severe case."

He had explained that another surgery was recommended. It was a solution that sounded like good news to her, and she felt a rush of relief. But then he had explained that the surgery would be a hysterectomy. Her symptoms would go away, her pain would be gone and she'd feel normal again. She'd have her life back, but— the kicker—she'd never have children.

But the surgery was her only option. She was infertile.

Emily and her mother had discussed the options long and hard. She had been in severe pain for the better part of a year. Her job was at stake. The school relied on her, and with her condition, she wasn't going to be able to continue teaching.

It had been the hardest decision she'd ever made, but she'd made it. The surgery had done all that the doctor had promised, and after a lengthy recovery, life had gone on, but there had always been a small part of her that quietly mourned the children she would never have.

"Is it possible that God has a different child in store for you?" her mother asked now.

Emily's heart constricted at those words, and she winced. "I've thought about it, Mom," she admitted, "but it would hurt. A lot. I'm crazy about Cora. Is that called bonding? I don't know. The thought of just giving her up to someone else and walking away makes my heart physically hurt."

Tears rose in her mother's eyes, and she nodded. "I know that feeling," she whispered.

Cora started to fuss, and Emily's mother passed the

baby to Emily. She tucked her little legs up underneath her and held her close the way Greg had done. Cora settled against Emily's chest and let out a contented sigh.

"That's a cute trick." Her mother chuckled. "Look at you!"

"Actually, Greg showed me this one." Emily blushed. "He's surprisingly good with kids."

"You seem to see quite a bit of him," her mother prompted.

Emily just shrugged.

"I don't believe that for a minute." Her mother laughed softly and folded her arms across her chest.

"We…" Emily paused, unsure of how to explain it. "Greg is great. I don't know what's happening, exactly."

"So something is happening?"

"Mom, stop it." Emily chuckled. "I don't know. To be on the safe side, I'd say that nothing at all is going on between us. We're friends."

Her mother nodded, but looked unconvinced. "He seems like a nice man."

A nice man. Yes, Greg was most definitely a nice man, and so much more. He was kind and compassionate. He was strong and solid; a guy with a veiled sense of humor and compassion when it mattered most. Emily looked lovingly down at Cora's downy head. Emily's mother looked down at her watch.

"I hate to rush out on you," she said, bending to kiss Cora. "But I've got to get back home. Your dad and I have a date."

"A date?" Emily raised her eyebrows with a grin.

"He's taking me out for dinner." Her mother let out a girlish laugh. "And I'm buying a new dress."

Emily laughed. "Go. Have fun. I'll be fine."

"Love you, Emmy," her mother said, blowing her a kiss. "You're doing just fine."

"I know." Emily chuckled. "Now go knock his socks off."

Her mother grabbed her keys from the counter and headed to the door. Turning back, she shot her daughter a playful grin. "I fully intend to!"

Later that evening, Emily sat in her big, overstuffed armchair, her feet tucked up underneath her. A novel lay on the arm of the chair, untouched. Cora slumbered in her bassinet, and Emily leaned her head back with a tired sigh. It had been a long day—the kind that reminded her that she was doing this on her own.

She'd honestly thought that having a large, supportive extended family would be a bigger help than it was. While she had lots of advice and plenty of offers to babysit, there was one thing she knew she was missing—someone to sit on the couch with at the end of the day. Someone to say, "Wow, what a day." Someone to share the memories with.

It would be nice to have a loving husband next to her during all of this, but she was no fool, either. If meeting the right guy was this hard when she was single without children, meeting Mr. Right just got a whole lot more complicated now that she was a single mom. How many guys wanted to jump into parenting with both feet? Not Greg.

She blushed at that thought. How come when she thought about husbands and marriage lately, Greg popped into her head?

As if on cue, the phone rang, and Emily looked around to try to spot the handset. It took her three rings to find it—this time in the bowl of fruit in the middle of her kitchen table. This lack of sleep was affecting her more than she liked to think.

"Hello?"

"Hi, it's Greg."

"Hi." Emily couldn't help but smile as she walked back toward her seat, but from the bassinet, she could hear Cora begin to fuss. It was the wet-diaper fuss—she could already tell the difference between whimpers. Pushing herself up from her chair, she went over to pick up the baby.

"How are you doing?" he asked.

"Pretty good." She bent over the bassinet and scooped Cora into her arms. "It's been a long day, though. It's tiring, you know?"

"You sound like you have it under control, though."

"I really do." She felt a little wave of pride as she looked around herself. "I mean, doing it alone is going to be a challenge, but I think I'm doing just fine."

"Good." She could hear the smile in his voice. "I guess I just wanted to check up on you."

"Professionally?" she teased, laying Cora down on the receiving blanket she had on the floor for this purpose.

"Not really." He laughed. "I can't find any professional excuse to call you at eight o'clock at night to say hi."

Emily blushed at that. "Well, it's nice all the same."

Cora wriggled as Emily pulled the wet diaper away, kicking her little legs happily at her new freedom. She wiped and cleaned and put on some more diaper cream, then Emily reached for a fresh diaper.

"Oh, no…"

"What's the matter?"

"Oh, it's okay."

"No, really. What's wrong?"

Emily closed her eyes for a moment and sighed. "For all my bragging about having it all under control on my own, I'm out of diapers."

"Completely out?" There was humor in Greg's voice.

"Yes." She fought back her rising irritation. She really did think she had it all under control, and suddenly she was faced with the frank reality that when problems came up, she was the go-to girl to take care of it. All of it.

"Do you need a hand?"

"No, it's okay. I'll do this on my own." She pushed herself up and looked around. "I guess I'll just have to put her back in the wet diaper and go pick up a new package. I'm sorry, sweetie," she cooed softly to the baby.

"Am I the sweetie?" Greg joked.

Emily just laughed.

"Let me pick you up some diapers," Greg said, serious now.

"I need to do this stuff on my own," she said. "I'll figure it out."

"Says who?"

Emily blinked at that. "I don't know…. My own stubborn pride?"

"Diapers come in different sizes, right?"

Emily smiled and shook her head. "She's just graduated to size two."

"I'll be there in twenty minutes," he said. "Can your pride take it?"

"It'll have to." Emily silently grimaced. "Thank you, Greg."

"No problem."

As she hung up the phone, Emily looked down at little Cora, still happily kicking her legs and enjoying the breeze.

"He's nice," Emily said in the singsong voice she often used with Cora. "Isn't he? He's a nice man...."

Cora seemed to agree.

Chapter Seven

By the time he arrived at Emily's house with a box of diapers in one hand, the moon loomed high and the air had cooled. Ringing the doorbell, he stood back to wait.

This is not professional, he told himself frankly. *What were you thinking?*

There was some rustling inside, then the door opened. Emily stood there with Cora on her shoulder, a washcloth covering the little bottom in a makeshift nappy.

"Hi." He felt a self-conscious smile come to his lips. "You look a little…um…wet."

"I am." She shot him a wry grin. "Thanks for coming, by the way." She stepped back to let him in. "Can I pay you back?"

"No, no." He carried the box in one hand and glanced around the living room, spotting her changing area.

"Really, I insist."

Greg glanced over at her. "No, don't worry about it."

She paused, and for a moment he thought she might argue the issue with him. Then a little smile tickled the corners of her lips. "Thanks. You know what?"

He raised his eyebrows inquisitively.

"I think we're officially friends." She laid Cora on

the blanket while he opened the box for her. "Don't you think?"

Greg laughed softly and shook his head. "It seems like it, doesn't it?"

Her response was a sparkling smile. "Thanks." She took the diaper he offered her.

After both the baby and Emily were changed, Emily led the way into the kitchen. She flicked on an electric kettle and pulled a tub of chocolate ice cream out of the freezer.

"I think we deserve a reward, don't you?" she asked.

Greg couldn't think of a reason why not, so he settled onto a stool by the counter and waited.

"So what do you do when you aren't working?" she asked.

"As in, for fun?" He grinned.

"Exactly." She dropped a spoon into a heaping bowl of ice cream and slid it across the counter toward him.

"I run five miles every morning," he said. "On days off, I like to golf, read...box."

"Box?" She turned around, eyebrows raised. "Seriously?"

He felt the heat rise in his face. "Is that completely Neanderthal?"

"Yes." She laughed softly. "When did that start?"

"When I was about ten, I got picked on a lot. I took an interest in boxing to protect myself at first, but I ended up really loving the sport."

"So..." She eyed him curiously. "You end up with black eyes and stuff?"

"No, no." He laughed. "We use helmets and gloves. It's a point system. I know how to hurt someone, but I don't want to actually do any damage."

Emily dropped a spoon into her own bowl and leaned against the counter as she took her first bite.

"What about you?" he asked. "What do you do for fun?"

"Well, I don't box." She shot him a grin. "I actually enjoy stargazing."

"Stargazing?" He eyed her in equal curiosity. "I didn't see that coming."

"My dad used to take me outside to look at stars when I was a kid. It started there. I like watching for meteor showers, or catching eclipses, just as a novice. I enjoy it. It reminds me how tiny I am."

He nodded thoughtfully. "I get that reminder a lot."

"Are you a Christian, Greg?"

"I am. Are you?"

She nodded. "So maybe you'll get it, too. I like to try to understand what's up there. It's almost like you can see God still creating when you see a star nebula. It's amazing. When you understand just how far apart stars really are, just how massive a tiny pinprick of light really is—it's staggering."

Greg took a taste of the creamy dessert, watching her thoughtfully. Her dark eyes stayed focused on her bowl as she swirled the spoon around, collecting the perfect bite. Her creamy complexion was set off by her dark hair sweeping her cheeks, and for a moment, he couldn't tear his eyes away from her. Emily Shaw was a deeper woman than he'd realized—and that intrigued him. A woman of intellect and faith…how often did one of those come around?

"Do you mind if I ask you something?" she said, raising her dark gaze to meet his.

"Sure."

"Why is it that you don't ever want kids of your own?"

There it was. This was the question that came up with pretty much every woman in his life, from his grandmother to women he was dating. They all wanted to know the same thing—why?

"In my experience, this never goes well." He eyed her cautiously. "I either sound heartless or stupid."

Emily's eyes crinkled up into a smile, and she turned toward the kitchen. "I find that hard to believe."

He frowned and looked down, trying to decide how much to say.

"I don't mean to pry," Emily said. "If you don't feel comfortable talking about it, that's okay. I was only curious."

"It's okay. My dad was a police officer, and he died in the line of duty."

"Oh, that's horrible. I think I remember that, but I was really young. What happened?"

The images came back, fuzzy memories from that fateful night. He'd been in bed, unable to sleep. The phone rang downstairs and he remembered the sound of his mother answering it, but something was wrong. Her tone changed, and she sounded frightened. He got out of bed and came downstairs to find her standing in the kitchen, the phone still in her hand and her other hand covering her mouth. That image of his mother—stunned, horrified, afraid—stayed with him.

"He was shot during an armed robbery. He stopped at a corner to pick something up and stumbled upon a robbery in process. The robber turned and shot him in the chest. The bullet entered just at the side of his bulletproof vest. He died at the scene."

Emily's expression was filled with sympathy. "How old were you?"

"Eight."

He'd been old enough to suspect that the reason his father stopped at that corner store was to pick up a candy bar for him. Greg had done well on his report card, and his dad had promised a chocolate bar as a reward. That report card still haunted him.

"I have my father's job, and it's dangerous," he said. "Haggerston isn't exactly known for its staggering crime rate—" Greg shot her a wry grin "—but with a job like this, danger is part of it."

"So you're afraid that something would happen to you and you'd leave a family behind." Emily pulled her glossy, dark hair out of her eyes.

"That about sums it up." He shrugged.

"It must have been tough growing up without your dad."

Tough didn't even begin to cover it. Greg had drawn the attention of a school bully. It was that bullying that sent him in search of some boxing lessons—a successful way to stop the bullying, once he learned what he was doing, but every miserable day of that year, he'd wondered what advice his dad might have given him. He had a feeling his dad would have had the solution— one that involved less fighting. He'd just died too soon to be of much use. Instead, Greg learned to use his fists more effectively than the bigger boy.

"Yeah, it was tough," he agreed, keeping his tone neutral. "School can be hard on a kid."

A flicker of understanding passed over her face. "Were you picked on?"

"Remember Richard Pike?"

She frowned. "Big guy, football team?"

"That's him. He made it his personal mission to make me miserable."

"Oh, Greg, that's awful."

He chuckled bitterly and waved it off. "I survived, but sometimes a kid just needs a dad to help out with these things. Bullying can crush a person, and childhood is hard enough without trying to take care of those kinds of problems alone. I learned how to box, and it helped, but I wouldn't want to leave some vulnerable kids behind if something were to happen to me in the line of duty."

She nodded. "I get it. I was close with my dad, too. Still am."

"Daddy's girl?"

"Afraid so. I remember how I used to be afraid of the dark, and he'd sing to me—'Twinkle, Twinkle, Little Star.' He said that God gave us stars so that we'd never be in the dark. No matter how dark it might seem, there was always at least one star to light our way. That was something that really stuck for me."

"That's sweet." A star to light his way—that wouldn't have been enough back when he was fighting off the bigger boys. He hadn't needed a far-off twinkle of light; he'd needed someone with bones and muscles to step in and protect him.

They were silent for a few moments, each in their own thoughts. Outside the kitchen window, the stars glittered like pale diamonds. The velvety night sky felt calm and vast, a comforting blanket of eternity outside the warmly lit kitchen.

Emily broke the silence. "So have you found out anything about Jessica?"

"I have. A little bit." Greg brought himself back to the present. "She worked as the manager of a clothing store. She graduated with high grades from college, and everyone seemed to think she was pretty talented. She lived in a little apartment above an Italian restaurant, and her finances were a wreck. She had several credit cards—the high-interest kind—racked up, and she'd been missing payments. Her credit score was in the dumps."

Emily nodded slowly, and he suddenly felt like a fool.

"I'm sorry. I'm probably being callous here. She's not a case—she's your cousin."

"No, it's okay." Emily gave him a sad smile. "A little bit of emotional distance is a good thing, if you can get it. Do you know anything about Cora's father?"

"No. I haven't gotten that far yet." He had to admit, that had piqued his curiosity, as well. "You don't know if she had a boyfriend or anything?"

"I have no idea." Emily shook her head. The kettle behind her started to whistle, and Greg moved toward it.

"I'll get that." He poured the water over the tea bag into the teapot, his mind moving over the case in his methodical way. The victim was young, college educated, but alienated from her family. She had a baby that no one knew about. She was on her way back to the town where the majority of her extended family lived when she had a head-on collision and was killed. She appeared to be distraught. She had a will where she left sole custody of her newborn baby to a cousin she hadn't spoken to in five or six years. There were a lot of gaps. Why did no one know about this baby?

"Well," Emily said as he poured her a cup of tea, "I have a feeling that you'll dig up some answers."

"Are you sure you want that?" Greg asked.

"What do you mean?"

"Sometimes the answers we look for don't bring the comfort we think they should."

Emily was silent for a moment, her eyes clouding in thought. "It's better to know, isn't it?"

"I tend to think so," he agreed. "I don't like surprises. I'm the kind of guy who likes to know what to expect."

"That makes two of us." She gave him a smile and lifted a spoonful of ice cream in a salute. "Here's to playing it safe."

Greg couldn't help but grin. Emily looked over at a pile of mail on the counter, and she stretched to reach it.

"I've been forgetting things," she admitted, shaking her head. "It's the lack of sleep. I put this here this afternoon and—" she looked up at the clock on the wall "—seven hours later I look at it?"

Greg tried to hide a smile as she sorted through the pile of letters. She stopped, the muscles around her eyes and jaw tightening.

"You okay?" he asked.

She tore open the envelope and grabbed the letter. Glancing over it, she let out a sigh. "Well, it looks like I have a court date."

"For the custody case?" Would it be too much to hope she had driven like a maniac past a traffic camera?

"Yes. I have three weeks."

That wasn't much time at all, but it was something. In three weeks, hopefully he'd be able to find a little more information for her about her cousin.

"That's plenty." Greg gave her what he hoped was a reassuring smile.

He just wished she looked more reassured.

Chapter Eight

The next afternoon, Greg got a call from Fran, a nurse at his mother's home, saying she was the most alert they'd seen her in weeks. His spirits immediately lifted. It had been so long since his mother had recognized him that the chance of being able to look into her face and have her see her son instead of a stranger was an exciting one. Making sure he was out of uniform first, he hopped into his car and headed down to the Shady Pines Nursing Home.

It was a squat building consisting of two wings. Fran stood there with a couple of other nurses, chatting while they filled out charts. She was a large lady in her fifties. Her dark-skinned face looked almost ageless, but her hands betrayed the years. When she saw Greg step inside, squinting from the bright sunlight, she raised a hand and hurried over.

"Thanks for calling, Fran."

"My pleasure. Go on over. You know where she is." Fran gave him a motherly pat on the arm. She had a son his age, and she tended to treat him like one of her own brood, a gesture that Greg privately appreciated.

As he made his way down the hallway, his shoes

squeaked on the newly polished linoleum. His mother's room was in the center of the west wing, a cozy little room with a pleasant view of the walking path many of the children used to get home from school. When he got to her door, he tapped softly and peeked inside.

"Hello?" His mother looked up at him, frowning. Her gray hair was freshly washed and combed, and she stood there, a small watering pot in hand, poised over her row of potted flowers on the windowsill.

"Hi." He could hear the hope in his voice, but he was afraid to alarm her.

She looked at him quizzically for a long moment, then set down her watering pot. "May I help you?"

"I was..." He paused. She didn't know him. She was certainly more together than she had been in a long time, but she wasn't in the present, that much was certain.

"You look an awful lot like my husband." She nodded. "Well. Imagine that. Did you know there are only a few different kinds of faces in the world? It looks like you got one quite similar to his."

"Could I come in for a few minutes?" Greg asked hopefully. "I just wanted to rest my feet."

"Oh, no." She shook her head. "I don't think that would be appropriate."

"Of course, of course," he assured her. "I only wanted to say hi. I'm a friend of your husband's."

"Then you know exactly how jealous he is, too." She laughed. Her laughter was light and cheerful. "Did you need something?"

"A glass of water would be great," he said, flashing her a grin. She sighed, heading toward the little sink in the corner of her room and taking down a plastic hospital-issue cup. Turning on the sink, she wagged a finger under the flow of water.

"This old house…" she muttered. "Always takes a bit to get cold water this time of year. It's always lukewarm."

He remembered that house well. The kitchen sink seemed to give you warm water when you wanted to drink it and cold water when you wanted to wash anything. It had driven his mother crazy, but after his father had passed away, she hadn't bothered getting it fixed. He thought it must have reminded her of when his dad was around, and she didn't want to lose the reminder. Now, in the hospital room, she was mentally changing the small room around her into the house from her memories.

"Thanks," he said as she handed him the cup. "This is kind of you."

"No bother," she said and turned back to her plants.

"So how are you?" he asked.

"I'm good, Mr…."

"I'm Greg."

"I have a five-year-old named Gregory." She smiled gently.

"What's he like?"

She looked over at him suspiciously. "Greg, let me be straight with you. My husband and I have an old-fashioned relationship. He's friendly with men, and I'm friendly with women."

"Oh, I understand," he said hurriedly.

"Are you married?"

"No." He shook his head.

"Well, then, I won't be of much interest to you. Thanks for stopping by. I'll tell my husband you came."

He was being dismissed. He stood there for a moment, looking at her hopefully. Would something trigger her memory? Would something flicker, some deep emotion somewhere? She looked back at him, an uncertain look on her face.

"Mom?"

"Pardon me?"

"Mom? It's me…."

The uncertainty turned to alarm on her weathered features, and he sighed. She didn't remember him. "Thank you, Mrs. Taylor. Give your husband my best."

Backing out of the room, he felt a lump rising in his throat. He took a deep breath, trying to push all the emotions out of sight. It had been getting worse and worse, her memories staying in the distant past for most of the time. This wasn't a good sign, and he knew it. If only she'd let him chat with her as a friend, at least then he could spend some time with her, but she kept dismissing him like some inappropriate flirt.

Fran came ambling down the hallway with a cart of medication squeaking cheerfully. She gave him a long, searching look.

"I'm sorry, honey," she said.

"I guess I missed the window." He gave her a shrug. "I'll drive faster next time."

"She was quite alert. She knew your dad was gone, and she thought you were a new police recruit. I thought for sure she'd recognize you." Fran shook her head. "Where was she now?"

"Dad was alive, and I was five."

She nodded. "That's a nice time for her. Well, next time, honey."

If there even was a next time.

"Thanks."

"Are you all right, Chief?"

"Oh, yes, I'm fine." He gave her a polite nod, covering the sadness that welled inside of him.

"You know, Chief," she said softly, putting a hand

on his arm. "On the other side, your mother is going to know what a loving son you were to her. She'll know."

"She's been getting worse, hasn't she?"

"I can't talk about that. I'm not the doctor—"

"I can tell." He sighed and pressed his lips together. "You know, what I wouldn't give to just hug my mother. But she won't let me."

"Now, that is a lady with boundaries!" Fran chortled, her eyes twinkling. Then she grew more serious, and her eyes filled with sympathy. "Come here, honey."

She opened her arms. Greg bent down and she wrapped her warm, soft arms around him, rocking him gently back and forth. He and Fran had become friends over the past couple of years that his mother was in Shady Pines, but they'd never hugged.

"I'm a mother with a boy your age," she said, nodding reassuringly. "I'll pass along this hug just as soon as she'll let me."

He closed his eyes for a moment, feeling the maternal love surrounding him. "You're a good boy, Greg," she said softly. "I know that your mother loves you. And you're taking real good care of her."

She released him and he stood up, a lump in his throat.

"Thanks, Fran."

"Anytime." She patted his hand and went back to her cart with the wobbly wheel, moving down the hallway toward the next door. He peeked back into his mother's room. She was watering the plants. With a sigh, he headed back down the hall toward the outside door and blinding sunlight. He'd do what he always did—go back to work.

"Seriously?" Emily stared at Beth in dismay. "What about a baby shower for *you?*"

They sat outside a little café, Cora sleeping in her car seat in the shade of the table's umbrella and two tall glasses of fruit smoothie between them. The day was warm and the drinks were chilled—the perfect combination for late June.

"I've got three months to go," Beth said with a faint shrug. "Everybody likes having the baby shower after the baby has arrived so they can ooh and aah over a little cutie."

"I know, but…" Emily sighed, letting her eyes rove out to the street, watching some pickup trucks navigate the four-way stop. "But this is terrible timing. I don't even know if Cora will be able to stay with me."

"I didn't tell them about that." Beth stirred her raspberry smoothie with the straw, her eyes on her drink. "I didn't think it was their business, and they were so eager to do this for you. We've both taught at that school for our entire careers. The other teachers feel a little protective. You can't blame them."

"Can't you cancel it?" Emily asked.

"Yeah, I'll tell them to cancel it. Sure." Beth nodded.

Emily sighed. She knew they were just trying to be supportive and kind. She'd been teaching at that elementary school for five years now, and the staff had a great camaraderie. Beth looked up, and Emily caught her eye.

"It's already planned, isn't it?" she asked.

"Yes." Beth blushed. "Mary Ellen is making the cake, and everyone has contributed one square for a quilt. Nancy is going to sew it up the night before the party. She's a pro when it comes to quilting."

"Oh, my goodness." Emily closed her eyes for a moment. "You are all so sweet."

"We know." Beth chuckled. "But no pressure, Em."

"What do you mean, no pressure?" Emily retorted.

"How can I tell them I'm not interested, especially when they've already put so much into this?"

"It was supposed to be a surprise party, but I talked them out of that," Beth offered.

Emily shot her friend a wry grin and took a sip of her watermelon-mint smoothie. She looked down at Cora, who lay happily in her car seat, wiggling her bare toes in the summer warmth.

"When is it?" Emily asked.

"In a couple of weeks." Beth reached over and put her hand over Emily's. "You can back out, Em. They'll understand. This is complicated."

"Maybe we could just put it off until after the hearing…." Emily watched as a woman across the street paused to look in a shop window, her toddler in a stroller, doing his best to squirm out. She smiled wistfully.

"Look," Beth said quietly. "We all know that this is complicated. This is a small town, and gossip travels faster than light. So don't blame me for gabbing, but everyone is well aware that it isn't all cut-and-dried."

"I know, I know. People will talk."

Cora let out a whimper, and Emily bent down to undo the straps of her seat and lifted the baby up onto her lap. Cora snuggled into Emily's arms contentedly, looking around herself with big blue eyes.

"We want to be here for you," Beth said. "I don't know how this will work out, but let's have some faith that God will leave the two of you together. In the meantime, you're a mom. Let us support you. That's what this is about—us taking care of you."

Emily couldn't help but smile. "I guess you have a point."

"So?" Beth asked cautiously. "Can we have the baby shower?"

Emily nodded. "Okay. You make a good argument." She took a long sip of her drink.

Beth grinned. "Excellent. Now find a date. It's a Jack and Jill."

Emily almost choked and coughed several times before she could catch her breath. "What?" she demanded.

"Oh, didn't I mention that before?" Beth asked innocently. "Well, think about Neil and Marcus."

Neil and Marcus were fellow teachers both women knew well.

"They'd want to be there, too," Beth continued, "and we can't very well allow them to come and not their wives...so you can see how it would get awkward if we didn't make it a Jack and Jill."

"You're telling me that on top of all this, I need a date?" Emily shook her head. "Beth, no!"

"What about Greg?"

"What about him?"

"Why not ask him to come as your Jack?"

Emily shot her friend a dry look and turned her attention to Cora, who was trying to suck on her tiny fist. "A date, huh?"

"Oh, I'm just being a pain." Beth chuckled. "Come alone or come with Greg. We'll love you either way."

Emily pointed her straw at Beth and narrowed her eyes teasingly. "You're pushing."

"Maybe a tad, but he's a sweet guy, and you have to admit that you've got a wee crush."

"A tiny one." Emily held up half an inch with her fingers. "But crushes are no excuse for hugely awkward social situations."

"Since when?" Beth asked. "There's no better excuse. But really, do what you want. Just come, okay?"

Emily grinned. "I'll be there."

The rest of the time they spent chatting about Beth's baby shopping, Cora's sleep patterns and Nina, considering she wasn't there to roll her eyes at them. When Beth announced it was time for her to go for her doctor's appointment, they hugged each other and headed off in opposite directions.

As she strapped Cora into her car seat, Emily heard her cell phone ringing in her purse. Pulling it out, she flipped it open as she tightened the last strap.

"Hello?"

"Hi, Emily." It was Greg. Emily couldn't help but smile.

"Hi. How are you?"

"Not bad. Say…I've dug something up, and I wanted to run it by you."

"Oh?" Emily straightened and pulled her fingers through her hair. "What did you find?"

"Can you think of any reason that Jessica would have had large deposits coming into her checking account the last few months?"

Emily was silent for a moment, processing his question. Large deposits? That sounded weird.

"How large are we talking?" Emily asked.

"Ten thousand and larger, each coming into her account on the first of the month, going back four months."

"Wow." She let out a sigh and closed the door, moving around to the driver's side. "I have no idea. You don't know where they were coming from?"

"Not yet. Would her parents have been giving her money?"

Emily's mind went to Uncle Hank. It didn't seem even remotely possible. "Her mom died, and her dad spent pretty much all they had on her hospital care. He's flat broke. He even lost the house. There's no way he could be giving anyone thirty or forty grand in cash."

"That's what I suspected."

Emily got into the driver's seat and started the vehicle, cranking the air-conditioning for Cora's benefit. Glancing back, Cora looked happy enough, looking around and attempting to chew on her little fist again.

"What does this mean?" Emily asked.

"I don't know, but it doesn't add up." Greg was silent for a moment. "So how are you doing?"

"Good." Emily flipped down the mirror. She looked tired. "Well, my friends at work are throwing me a baby shower."

"That sounds nice."

"It is…and it isn't." Emily wondered if he'd understand what she was about to explain. "I don't know what's going to happen, and celebrating all of this might be a bit premature."

"I get that." His voice was quiet and comforting. "So what are you going to do?"

"Beth convinced me." She chuckled. "She's awfully convincing when she wants to be."

"Oh?"

"I can blame her for more than one fashion mistake." Emily rolled her eyes. "But her heart is in the right place. What can I do?"

Greg just laughed.

"There is one complication…." Emily closed her eyes and silently grimaced. Should she even ask?

"What's that?"

"It's a Jack and Jill."

"Meaning?"

"Nothing. Don't worry about it."

"No, I was serious." He chuckled. "What does that mean? I'm a man. I'm not up on baby-shower etiquette."

"It means that men and women will come. Mainly, it means that women will bring their husbands and boy-friends."

"Ah…" There was humor in his voice. "You need a Jack?"

"That would help immensely." She had to smile. "Thank you, Greg. I really appreciate this."

"So do I need to bring you a corsage or something?" he joked.

"No, pretty much just show up. And I'll be eternally grateful."

"Oh, I don't need eternal gratitude." He laughed. "It'll be fun."

"If I can ever do anything for you, Greg, let me know."

There was something muffled in the background. "…yes, thanks…. No, four of them. Oh, Joyce? Can I get some copies of these, too?"

"Busy?" Emily asked.

"Yeah, I'd better get going. I'll get those party details from you later, okay?"

"Okay. See you."

As she hung up the phone, she couldn't help but smile to herself. Looking back at Cora again, she gave the baby a smile.

"Ready to go home?" she asked.

Cora blinked and pulled some glistening fingers from her mouth.

"Me, too," Emily said, and put the vehicle in gear and pulled out onto the street.

Chapter Nine

A few days later, Emily stood in her parents' living room, the diaper bag at her feet. Glancing at her watch, she mentally calculated how much time she had before she'd be late. Her mother cooed and babbled to Cora, lifting the baby into her arms.

"Oh, we'll be just fine, Em," she said. "Won't we, Cora? Won't we?"

Emily chuckled, watching her mother making a fishy face for Cora's benefit. "Okay, I have three bottles. You won't need all of them, but I have an extra, just in case. I think she's growing, and she's been hungry lately. The diapers will definitely be enough, but make sure you use the diaper cream. Her bottom has been sensitive lately. Also…"

"Sweetheart," her mother said, looking up pointedly. "You've already told me all of this. Don't worry. I raised you, you know."

"I know." Emily bent down and kissed Cora's plump cheek. Only a few weeks ago, Cora had been much thinner. She was growing and getting nicely plump, and Emily felt a swell of personal pride in those rolls and dimples. She was doing something right.

"We'll be fine," her mother repeated, giving her a re-assuring smile. "Okay? Have a good time."

Emily wasn't exactly going out for a good time. She had a dentist appointment, and then needed to make a quick stop by the drugstore to get a few toiletries. It would be the first time she'd gone out without Cora since the baby had arrived, and it felt strange.

As she walked out the front door toward her wait-ing vehicle, her father came around the house holding a garden hose. His iron-gray hair was neatly cropped in a fresh cut, and he wore a tattered yellow golf shirt. He loved that old shirt, and the only way her mother let him keep it was if he promised to wear it only when doing yard work.

"Hi, Emmy," he called. "Off so soon?"

"I have a dentist appointment."

"Look what I found." He held up an old telescope, covered in dust. Emily stopped and squinted, looking more closely.

"You still have that?" she asked. "When did you get me that?"

"You were seven. You said you'd outgrown 'Twinkle, Twinkle, Little Star,' and I bought you this to look at the real thing." He gave her a wistful smile. "I just found it in the garage. I thought maybe we could show Cora the stars one day."

Tears misted Emily's eyes, the memories flying back. She'd been seven going on fourteen, as they said, and she remembered how disappointed her father had been when she declared herself officially grown-up and no longer in need of his silly songs.

"I think we've got some time before Cora is old enough for telescopes," she said.

"Well, I'll just get it ready." He dropped the hose in

a pile beside the outside faucet and wiped some of the dust off the old telescope with the palm of his hand.

"Dad?"

He looked up at her cheerfully. "Yes?"

"I have a court date for Cora's custody hearing."

The sparkle went out of his eyes, and his shoulders slumped just a little. He gave a quick nod. "Oh, that. Just a bit of red tape. It'll be fine."

"Do you think so?" She didn't know what she expected him to say. He didn't know any more than she did.

"I think so." He nodded thoughtfully. "I'll start cleaning this up." He lifted the dusty telescope in a salute.

She felt like hugging her old father then. He was so determined, so stubborn when it came to letting go of hope, and that was part of what she loved about him.

"I'll see you, Dad." She gave him a grateful smile and pulled open the door of her vehicle. He didn't know any more about this than she did, and he had no possible way to see the future, but somehow her father's opinion made all the difference.

As she drove down the road toward the dentist's office, her mind kept going back to that old telescope. When she'd turned seven, she'd decided that the second grade was too advanced for silly little songs like "Twinkle, Twinkle, Little Star," and she'd informed her father that she would just have to grow up. She could still remember the look on his face when she said it—a mixture of sad tenderness and indulgence.

"I'll tell you what, princess," he'd said. "You're right. You are very grown-up now. I think you're grown-up enough to look at some real stars, don't you?"

Looking back on it now, he hadn't been willing to lose their little tradition together, even if it meant evolving it a little, and she was grateful for that. She had countless warm memories of standing with her father in their backyard, looking through that rickety little telescope at a full moon, or at a cluster of stars while he told her about the galaxies and nebulae beyond. As they looked at the craters in the moon, their conversation would move to other subjects: the girl who ignored her at school, her insecurity over her big feet, her curiosity about family stories she wasn't old enough to know yet. She might have thought she was very grown-up, but her daddy still knew how to comfort her.

The dentist's visit took longer than she'd expected. By the time Emily was driving back to her parents' house, her mouth partially frozen, two hours had passed. The warm wind came in through the open window, and a jangly tune played on the radio—something about a brokenhearted cowboy.

Her parents lived on a quaint little street with small, boxy houses built in the sixties. They were cute in the way Lego houses were cute, with shutters and steeply sloped roofs, a garage off the side and a mailbox out front. She could drive down this street without even thinking, and it almost felt as if the car knew the way. Pulling into her parents' drive, she saw the little BMW parked in front of her, and her heart sank. It belonged to her cousin Steve.

"Shoot," she muttered to herself. She parked her SUV next to it and got out, slamming the door. "What now?"

The screen door was closed, but the main door to the house was open, letting a warm breeze come inside. Emily could hear their voices before she even opened the screen, and when she did, the chitchat silenced. Stepping into the living room, she saw Sara sitting in the easy chair, Cora snuggled in her arms and Steve standing protectively over her.

Sara wore her hair pulled away from her face with a headband, a look both too young for her and also oddly appropriate. She looked more like a slender schoolgirl sitting there, except for her hands. Her hands moved with the experience of a mother, confident and accustomed to babies.

"Hi," Emily said.

"Hello, Emily," Sara said sweetly. "How was the dentist?"

"Oh, fine." Emily touched her face. "A couple of cavities. How are you doing?"

"I missed her." Sara looked up bashfully. "You've got to forgive me, but I had to come and get some good snuggles in."

There was nothing wrong with coming to cuddle a baby, but something inside of Emily piqued at that. Sara looked back down at Cora lovingly, making wide-eyed faces at her.

"Such a pretty girl," Sara cooed. "Such a pretty, pretty girl. Yes, you are."

Steve looked over at Emily silently.

"How are you, Steve?" Emily asked, going over to collect the baby bag. It sat next to the chair, tucked behind Sara's purse as if it were part of her things.

"Oh, leave that," Sara said, gently swatting Emily's hand as she went to reach. "I might need a cloth or something."

Emily stopped for a moment, then reached past her and took the bag. Sara ignored her, her attention on the baby.

"So are you enjoying your summer off?" Steve asked brightly.

"Absolutely," Emily replied. "One of the perks of my job."

"But September comes up soon enough…." He looked at her levelly. "Before you know it, this summer adventure will be over and you'll be back in the saddle."

Emily frowned. Why did she feel like a teenager being lectured about responsibility? What she did with her career was strictly her business, in her opinion, and she resented her cousin's meddling. "Do you have any plans for the summer?" she asked instead.

Sara looked up at Steve, and they exchanged a look.

"Not really." Steve shrugged. "We like to keep the girls pretty close to home. Family time is precious."

Emily glanced at her watch. She didn't actually have any pressing appointments, but she wasn't comfortable with this visit. The tension in the room, despite the cheery smiles, could be played with a guitar pick.

"Thanks for watching her, Mom." Emily turned toward her mother, who stood there with a nervous expression on her face. They exchanged a baffled look.

"No problem, sweetie," her mother said smoothly. "Anytime."

"I'd better get going." Emily adjusted the baby bag on her shoulder and picked up the car seat from where she'd left it by the door.

When Sara made no move to hand Cora over to Emily, her mother stepped in.

"Sara," Emily's mother said softly, moving toward the door as if to block an escape. "Emily is Cora's guardian. We have to respect her wishes for Cora."

"Cora needs time with me," Sara replied, giving them a chilly smile. "She needs to know who I am." She pulled the baby in closer and turned herself away from them as if to put her body between the baby and everyone else.

Emily looked up at Steve, who glanced away uncomfortably. "What is going on, exactly?"

"Sara, let's not make a scene here," Steve murmured.

"I'm not done yet." Sara's expression was near panic. "She needs to know me."

"Why are you saying this?" Emily asked quietly. Cora began to squirm, looking around, then she opened her mouth in a thin wail.

"Shh, shh." Sara stood up and began to bounce the baby gently in her arms.

"Thanks, Sara," Emily said. "I'll just take her now."

"This is better for Cora," Sara said, reluctantly letting Emily take the baby from her arms. "What do you think it's going to be like for her when she comes home with us? She needs to know who I am."

Emily fought down the anger rising up inside of her. Cora nestled cozily into her arms, happy now that she was with Emily, but Sara still stood there, her eyes full of tears and her gaze locked on the baby.

"She needs to know I'm here."

Steve put a hand firmly on her shoulder, and Sara clamped her mouth shut.

"I'm pretty sure our lawyers would advise us to stop these emotionally charged meetings," Emily said, her voice low. "Look, we're family. We shouldn't be going to court, but it is what it is. Let's not make anything worse here today. We have three weeks till our court date. Perhaps we should just keep our distance until then."

"That's probably a good idea," Steve agreed quickly. "Come, Sara, we need to go pick up the girls."

With a lingering look at little Cora, Sara stood up and adjusted her dress primly. "Thanks for the tea, Aunt Rita. We'd better go pick up the girls. They'll be missing us by now."

Steve and Sara walked to the front door, hesitated a moment and then opened it.

"Thanks again." Steve's voice was unnaturally high, then they stepped outside and the screen banged shut behind them. Emily and her parents stood in silence until they heard the little BMW start and pull out of the drive.

"Wow." Her mother sighed. "What was that?"

Emily just shook her head. "They seem pretty confident."

Her mother grimaced and shook her head. "Well, they shouldn't be counting their chickens."

Emily's father stood by the kitchen door, his lips pressed firmly together in a thin line. When he felt Emily's eyes on him, he looked over at her, his expression unchanged.

"Should I be worried?" Emily asked, her energy draining out of her. She knew what she was hoping for. She wanted her father to tell her that it wasn't as bad as it looked—that it was really just normal family tensions around a time like this. His expression, however, suggested otherwise.

"You should ask the chief of police about that," he said. "He'd know, and I'd feel better if you talked it over with him. At least have it on record that your cousins are acting strangely."

"That was definitely weird, right?" She looked from her mother's stricken face back to her father.

"Downright loony," her father said. "Call Chief Taylor."

Greg sat in his car outside Shady Pines Nursing Home. He wasn't ready to go in yet. He was relatively sure what he'd meet with, and he wasn't ready for the rejection yet. A man never thought he'd live to see the day that his own mother would forget him. It hurt deep down in a place that ached like a punch in the gut. He just needed his mother to recognize him…to let him comfort her.

She'd never been the type to let him comfort her, though. Even at his father's funeral, his mother was stoic and composed. He remembered standing next to her, and her spine had been like steel. She didn't bend— not once. She'd stared at the casket, deep sadness swimming in her eyes, but her face was like a granite mask. It had taken three years for her to smile again, but she'd never cried in front of him, either. His mother had been a rock, brave and immovable.

"Your dad is gone," she'd told him gently the night that they'd buried him. "And we'll take care of each other now. But don't worry—you've got a pretty tough mama. We'll be all right."

That had been her motto—he had a pretty tough mama. Looking back on it now, he could see her struggle to be both mother and father to him, but at the time he'd been confused by the change in her. He could still remember the day he'd come home with a nasty black eye from a boxing class that he hadn't been able to hide. When she'd got home from work, she'd stopped in the process of taking off her coat.

"What happened to you?" she'd demanded, bending down to look into his battered face. Her coat was still half-on.

"I fell," he lied.

"Where?" She gingerly touched his blue-smudged cheek with her cool fingers.

"Down a big hill." If she'd pressed further, he was relatively certain his lie would crumble around him. Instead, she gave him a long look, straight into his eyes and into his soul, if that were possible.

"That's quite the hill," she said softly. "I think I need to talk to your principal. Who did this to you?"

"Mom, don't embarrass me!" His anger erupted. "Quit treating me like a baby. I said I fell!"

As she pulled herself erect, he thought for a brief moment that she might cry, but she didn't. Instead, she calmly took off her coat, sucked in a deep breath and said, "Put some ice on that. It'll help with the swelling."

Whether she suspected he was spending his afternoons in a boxing ring, he never did know. He hadn't wanted her to know, and she hadn't pressed him after that.

Greg's phone rang and he looked down at it, preparing to screen the call. But when he saw that it was Emily, he picked it up.

"Hi," he said.

"Hi, Greg. How are you doing?"

"All right. How about you?" He could hear the terseness in his own voice. It wasn't intended, but he had a lot on his mind.

"I was hoping to talk to you about something...." She seemed to ignore or forgive his tone and pressed on.

"What's up?"

"I left Cora with my parents while I went out for a little while and, well..." She paused. "...something strange happened."

"With your parents?"

"Steve and his wife came to my parents' house while I was gone. I don't know how they knew Cora was there, but they found out somehow and—"

"What happened?"

"I don't know how to explain it." Emily sighed into the phone. "Sara didn't want to give Cora back to me. She kept saying that Cora needed to know her."

Greg opened his glove box and pulled out a form. This was definitely going to need to go on file as an incident. He jotted down the details as she gave them to him, telling the story of the strange meeting.

"What time was this?" he asked.

"Just now. Fifteen minutes ago."

He looked at his watch. It was almost two in the afternoon, so he made a note.

"Do I need to worry about this?" Emily asked. "I need to know honestly."

"I don't know." He sighed. "It was definitely strange behavior, and it would seem that your cousin's wife is getting a little unstrung over all of this."

"In her defense, she isn't normally like this."

"Well, stressful situations bring on uncharacteristic behavior." He filled in the last of the form and made a mental note to have it filed once he got back to the office. "I've got an incident report here that I just filled out. I'll need you to come by and sign it. It's the first step. If anything else happens, we'll have a trail to prove harassment if we need to."

"I don't want to sue my cousins." There was a tiredness in her voice as she said the words, and he could understand where she was coming from, but she hadn't seen all the things he'd seen, either.

"They're already suing you, remember?" He paused, waiting for a response, but when he didn't get one he added, "Do you want to come by and sign it?"

"I could come now."

"I'm not at the office, actually. I'm—" He stopped. This was personal. Did he really want to share this? The old cop self-reliance welled up inside of him.

"Oh, it's okay." Her voice was soft. "I'll come by when you're in the office."

Greg closed his eyes and pressed his lips together. Letting out a long breath, he opened his eyes again. "Emily?"

"Yes?"

"Do you feel like doing me a favor?"

"Sure. What do you need?"

When Emily drove into the Shady Pines parking lot, Greg got out of his car and waited for her to park in the space next to him.

He heard the creak of the emergency brake as she parked, and as she hopped out of the truck he was struck by how fresh she looked. Her cheeks were flushed, and her dark hair was swept back in a ponytail. She wore a mauve linen blouse that covered her modestly, showing only the barest hint of her collarbone.

"I didn't realize your mom was here, Greg," she said as she pulled open the backseat door and leaned in to pull out little Cora. He caught his eyes moving over the soft swell of her hips, and he pulled them back. Now was not the time to ogle.

"She's been here for a couple of years now, but it's been getting worse." He shook the form in his hand. "I should get you to take a look at this report and sign it, if you could."

"Oh, of course." She emerged with Cora and handed him the car-seat handle in exchange for the form and pen. Pursing her lips, she scanned it, then signed the bottom. "That looks about right."

"You'll want to give your lawyer a copy of that."

"Really?" She looked up uncertainly. "Wouldn't that make things a bit ugly?"

"He doesn't have to use it, but forewarned is forearmed."

She nodded. "I see your point." Taking her copy of the form, she tucked it in her purse. "So tell me about your mom."

"Her first name is Laura, and I don't know what time we'll catch her in. She's been going back farther and farther in time. The last time I was here, she thought I was a little boy still...or at least she thought she had a little boy, and I was just some threatening man as far as she was concerned." He gave her a wan smile, and they ambled slowly toward the main doors.

"Oh, Greg." Emily looked up at him sympathetically. "That has to hurt."

"She was gorgeous, my mom. I mean, really stunning. I'll have to show you a picture one of these days. So when she was young, she used to be pretty standoffish with other men. I can't get anywhere close to her."

Emily nodded. "What do you want me to do?"

"Just..." He paused and shrugged. "Talk to her? I don't know. She'll trust you."

"How do you know?"

"I just do." So much had changed with his mother since her diagnosis of Alzheimer's, but some things hadn't—like her impeccable judgment of character.

"Okay," she said.

When they came to the main doors, Fran looked up from the nurse's station and waved them through with a broad smile. She shot Greg one look of unabashed curiosity, but he flatly ignored it.

The inside of the nursing home was dim compared to the bright summer sunlight outside, and it took a few moments for his eyes to adjust. As they reached his mother's room, Emily looked up at him questioningly.

"Are you sure you're okay with this?" Greg asked.

"I was about to ask you the same thing." She chuckled softly. "I'm fine, Greg."

"No pressure."

"I know. I want to help, if I can."

Tapping on the door, Emily eased it open a little.

"Come in," a wavery voice called.

As they stepped inside, Greg could see his mother sitting in her little chair by the window, her Bible open in her lap.

"Oh, hello," his mother said uncertainly. "Can I help you?"

"Hi, I'm Emily." She stopped in the doorway. It was a respectful gesture, and Greg was grateful for it.

"Hello. Are you from the neighborhood?"

"Yes," Emily said. "I just thought I'd stop in and say hi."

"Come on in and have some tea," his mother said, giving her a smile. "Forgive me for not standing, but once I get down, in my condition it's hard to get back up again."

"Oh, don't worry," Emily said, stepping inside. "I'm Emily."

"I'm Laura. Why am I here? I don't remember why I'm here. Is this a hospital?"

"Sort of…" Emily glanced up at Greg.

"Because of the baby?" her mother asked. "I'm due in October." She gave a shy smile.

Greg felt a surge of sadness. She was farther back in time now, back to her pregnancy.

"I just thought I'd stop in and say hi." Emily gave a small shrug. "Congratulations. You must be so excited about the baby."

"I am." His mother blushed and looked away. "Tony will be back soon, I'm sure."

"This is Greg," Emily said, then stopped, sensing a

mistake. It didn't seem to faze his mother, though. The old woman rubbed a hand over her stomach.

"It's overwhelming, isn't it? I'm going to be someone's mother."

Emily nodded. "I still can't get over that." She laughed softly. "This must be your first?"

His mother nodded tiredly, a smile on her lips. "Our very first. I'm positive it's a boy."

Greg couldn't help but grin, and he attempted to hide it behind his hand. In her mind, she was pregnant with him.

"Do you know what you'll name him?"

Greg's gaze flickered toward Emily's face, but she didn't look in his direction at all. Her entire attention was focused on his mother.

"I like Ernest." His mother smiled. "That's my father's name. But my husband wants to name him Gregory." Her eyes moved over to Greg, and she frowned slightly.

"I like them both," Emily said quietly. "I guess you'll know when you see him."

His mother's eyes flickered toward him again, and her frown deepened. He tensed. Was it coming—the confusion, the anger?

"Your husband looks a lot like my husband," his mother said, looking at Greg more closely. "Isn't that strange...."

"Do I?"

"Well." She batted her hand, letting it fall back onto her stomach. "They say there are only so many faces in the world, and we have to share them around."

Greg nodded, relaxing. She said the same thing to him every time he visited. It was almost comforting.

Cora squirmed in the car seat, and his mother looked down at her.

"She's adorable," his mother said. "What's her name?"

"Cora."

"That's pretty. I really like it."

The women were getting along splendidly, and Greg couldn't help but smile watching them chat. The fear and shouting that normally surrounded his visits didn't seem to be coming, but he wasn't sure if it was safe to feel relieved yet. It was all talk about babies, but he could see his mother relaxing and looking happy. So this was what she'd been like when she'd been a young woman. Couple that sweet personality with her looks, and he could see why his father had asked her to marry him after two weeks. She was a catch.

"It's very nice of you to come visiting with your wife," his mother said, turning toward him. "And you two have such a beautiful baby."

"Thank you." Greg grinned, glancing at Emily. A small blush had risen in her cheeks, and he thought it suited her.

"What do you do?" she asked politely.

Before thinking better of it, he said, "I'm a cop."

"So is Tony." A rare smile broke over her lined face. "Imagine that. Well, this has turned out very well. Emily and I will have someone who understands while we worry about our husbands."

"I think we'll be good friends." Emily reached across and took his mother's wrinkled hand. "Maybe I could come by again, and we'll visit."

"I'd like that." She smiled back. "I wonder when Tony will be here. If you see him, Greg, please tell him his wife is asking about him."

His mother smiled wistfully, and for the first time

Greg froze, watching that expression on her aged features. It had been a long time since he'd seen his mother smile like that—a good twenty-five years. She had her husband back.

"You and Tony seem really happy," Greg said.

"Madly in love," she replied, a twinkle in her eye. "It was nice to meet you both. I'll let Tony know you stopped by. Emily and Greg, right?"

Emily nodded and stood up. As she rose, his mother pushed herself from her chair.

"It was wonderful to meet you," Emily said, and she leaned forward and wrapped her arms around his mother, giving her a gentle squeeze. His mother looked surprised at first, then she smiled and squeezed Emily back.

Tears misted Greg's eyes, and he turned away to hide it. By the time he looked up, Emily was ready to go.

"Come on by, Emily, anytime at all," his mother called. "Goodbye, Greg."

As they stepped outside the room, Greg felt a surge of relief. He'd been waiting for everything to fall apart on them, for his mother's confusion to come back, for her fear to turn into anger. Her voice would rise in pitch, and she'd point a finger at him, shaking in fury. "Get out! Get out!" It hadn't happened, not this visit, and he was grateful. Emily looked up at him, her eyebrows raised. "Was I okay?"

"You were great." He heard the catch in his voice, and he cleared his throat. When he looked back into his mother's room, he saw her resettled in her chair with the Bible back on her lap. She'd always been a woman of faith, and even when her mind was confused, he was glad she had that comfort.

"Are you okay?" Emily asked quietly.

"I'm great, too." He smiled. "You hugged her."

"Of course."

"She hasn't let me hug her in over a year."

Emily's face suddenly fell, and she shook her head. "Really? Oh, wow. I had no idea. I'm sorry if I..." She didn't seem to know how to finish the sentence.

"No, don't apologize." They walked back down the hall. He resisted the urge to look back again toward her room. "If it can't be me, I'm glad someone is hugging her. She needs hugs."

Risking a look down at Emily as they reached the outside door, he saw tears in her eyes, and then they broke out into the summer sunlight. He took a deep breath of fresh air.

"Thanks," he said, clearing his throat again. "I appreciate this."

"What are friends for?" She put her cool fingers on his arm. Her hand felt comforting there—more than comforting, if he had to be brutally honest. She sparked something inside of him that made him want to pull her closer, run his fingers through her dark, glossy waves...

He pulled his eyes away from the pinkness of her lips, just parted. She didn't seem to notice. Instead she said, her voice low and quiet, "And for the record? Your mom raised a very sweet son."

Greg felt a smile come to his lips. "Want a coffee?"

"I'd love one."

Cafe au Lait was one of the last local coffee shops left in Haggerston, hunched on the corner of Main Street and Fourth Avenue, across the street from the library. Emily sat in front of an iced cappuccino while Greg sipped a regular coffee, black.

"How long has your mom been sick?" Emily asked.

"For a few years. It started with her forgetting special dates, like her grandchildren's birthdays, that sort of thing. Then when people reminded her, she'd claim she hadn't forgotten at all. There were a lot of hurt feelings. Especially since my sister lives out in Cincinnati, so figuring it out long-distance wasn't easy."

"I could see that."

"I realized something was wrong when she called me to take her grocery shopping, and when I arrived, she'd completely forgotten. I mean, completely. She demanded to know why everyone was trying to make her feel bad all the time. I got her a doctor's appointment for the next week." Greg tapped two sugar packets against his palm, then tore them open. "A couple of years ago, she had to come to this nursing home. We couldn't take care of her anymore. Not safely."

"Was she mad?" Emily asked.

"Furious." He shot her a grin. "My mother always was a tough woman, and when she was angry, she was a force of nature."

Emily laughed softly. "I know the type."

"But she'd lock herself outside, wander around her neighborhood in her nightgown. It wasn't safe anymore."

"That has to be hard."

The spoon clinked against the side of Greg's cup as he stirred. "Well, you do what you have to."

Late-afternoon sunlight poured through the window, warming her arms despite the air-conditioning. Emily took a sip of her sweet, icy drink.

"Your mom seems like a neat lady."

Greg smiled. "She is. She doesn't know me anymore, though."

"I'm sure she never thought she'd live to forget her

child." Emily looked into Greg's sad face. He nodded slowly.

"I really appreciate your help today."

"You've been doing this alone, haven't you?" she asked.

He chuckled. "Am I that obvious?"

She shrugged. "You're that kind of guy. Capable. Responsible. Stubborn."

He shot her a grin at her last descriptor. "I guess I've always been the one people came to for help." He lifted his cup to his lips. "Being chief of police around here plays into it."

"So who do *you* lean on?" she asked.

"God."

She smiled at that. "Which human being, then?"

Greg shook his head. "I take care of it myself."

"Everyone needs someone to lean on."

He was silent for a long moment, then smiled. "I suppose one day I'll find someone to rely on. Can't say I'd ever lean on her, though. But it would be nice to share things."

"She might end up being stronger than you think," Emily said with a soft laugh.

"Everyone is strong if they have to be," he agreed. "But I need to be the strong one. I just can't seem to help my mom." He sighed. "Sometimes being the strong one isn't enough. Sometimes that just scares her."

"And you hate having someone else help her when you can't."

He smiled. "Normally, yes, but it's different with you."

"How?"

"You're—" he paused, shrugged "—hard to resent."

Emily burst out laughing. "That's a good thing."

He nodded. "Definitely."

The waitress came by with a pot of hot coffee. She tucked her pad of paper into her apron and lifted the pot.

"Warm you up, Chief?" she asked.

Greg lifted his cup for a refill.

"You want pie? Cake?" she asked as she poured.

"This place has the best cherry cheesecake. Have you had it?" Greg asked, fixing Emily with a mischievous smile.

Emily shook her head. "Not yet."

"Could we get two pieces?" Greg asked, holding up two fingers.

"We only have one piece left," she said with a wink. "But don't worry—I'll bring two forks."

Before they could object, the waitress whisked away from the table, heading across the café to another table, her coffeepot held aloft.

Greg chuckled and shook his head. "It's worth it. You'll love this cheesecake."

The bell above the door tinkled, and Greg turned to see who came inside. He raised a hand in a wave.

"This is Benny, one of the officers at the station."

"Hi, Chief," the big man said with a grin. He ambled over to where they sat and pulled up a chair. "Hey, it's Sweet pea."

Emily grinned as he bent over the car seat and made a face for Cora's benefit. "Hi there, Sweet pea," he crooned. "You're looking good, kiddo. Growing right up."

"This is Emily," Greg said.

Benny shot out a hand and shook hers with enthusiasm. "Nice to meet you."

"Likewise." She nodded down at Cora. "Do you want to hold her?"

"Sure do." A grin split his face as Emily lifted the baby into his arms.

"Here we go," the waitress sang out as she deposited a large wedge of cheesecake onto the middle of the table. "And forks."

She put two forks down, then looked at Benny dubiously. "An extra fork?" She held out a third fork questioningly.

"Thanks." Benny took the proffered fork and beamed at Greg. "You're a peach, boss."

Greg rolled his eyes, but pulled the plate out of Benny's reach. "Hey, ladies first. Let her try this."

Emily took a forkful of cheesecake, and when she put it into her mouth, she couldn't help but sigh with pleasure. Creamy, tangy, topped with cherries… It was perfection.

"Right?" Greg grinned.

She nodded. "Amazing."

"Boss, I know this is your day off, but—" Benny suddenly blanched. "Oh, man. It's your day off, and you're with a woman eating cheesecake—" He looked from Greg to Emily, his face reddening. "You're on a date."

"No!" Emily and Greg blurted out at once.

"Just chatting," Emily said. "You're more than welcome to join us."

Benny looked at Greg, who didn't answer.

"I actually should get going," Benny said slowly, eyes still on Greg. "Yep, definitely need to move along."

Emily laughed. "It was nice to meet you, Benny."

"Same here, ma'am." Benny handed Cora back, giving her a wink. "He's kind of gruff and he acts like a big toughie, but the chief is a decent guy."

"Move along, Benny," Greg retorted drily.

Benny chuckled. "See you." Pushing himself to his feet, he headed for the door.

Emily stifled a laugh behind her hand.

"Yeah, that's the raging respect I get around the station," he joked.

"Oh, it's obvious he really likes you." Emily smiled. "Your officers trust you."

He nodded. "And I trust them. That's the kind of ship I run."

Emily looked at her watch. "I have an appointment with my grandma. I'm helping her book some vacation tickets. I'd better not leave her waiting too long."

Greg smiled. "Sure."

"It was nice to just talk, though. I liked this."

"Me, too." He chuckled. "Sorry about Benny."

"Oh, he's harmless."

"And thanks." His tone became more guarded, and he broke eye contact. "For today. It meant a lot."

Emily nodded and cleared her throat. "Anytime."

The moment had passed. His smile turned professional, and he gave her a nod.

"Take care," he said.

As she left the coffee shop, car seat in one hand, Emily heaved a sigh. Greg was a man with such depth and strength, but he used that strength to maintain his solitude.

Everyone needed someone to lean on, she thought as she unlocked her car. Men might like to think they were invulnerable, but she knew better. Not every woman needed rescuing, either. While he appreciated her help, she could feel his resistance.

Greg had been holding everything together on his own for so long that Emily felt sure it had become a habit for him. He was the strong one, the rescuer, the knight in shining armor for the whole town of Haggerston.

Emily didn't need Greg to be a knight on a white horse, but she did wish some of his walls would come down and that their friendship would deepen.

Maybe that was too much to ask.

Chapter Ten

Monday lunch with Beth and Nina was a tradition. They met at their favorite spot, Lou's Diner. It didn't look like much on the outside, complete with a big glowing sign that only lit up the *L* and *U,* but Lou's had the best salads in town, hands down. They sat in a booth at the back, Cora sleeping soundly in her car seat on the bench beside Emily, and Nina and Beth on the other side facing her. Past the little wire basket of ketchup, mustard and sugar packets, she could see the parking lot out the window. Not much of a view, but this booth just about had their names on it. Monday lunch, the servers always kept it available. Nina's generous tips probably had a lot to do with that.

Emily looked down at Cora. Her big blue eyes were open now, and she looked at one of her tiny clenched fists, nearly going cross-eyed in the effort. Emily ran her fingers over Cora's silky red curls. As she looked up again, she heard the ding of the bell over the front door and glanced over to see Greg stepping inside. He was in uniform, his hat tucked under one arm in a way that drew her attention to just how defined those biceps were. He squinted from the summer sunlight, and as he came into the dimmer interior, he paused for a moment, resting the heel of his hand on the heavy belt that held his gun, badge and pepper spray. Emily thought she'd veiled her reaction, but apparently not, because Beth and Nina both turned to look where Emily's attention had gone.

Greg gave her a grin and raised a hand in hello. Emily felt the blush rising in her cheeks.

"I'm sorry, Em, but I don't have much time before I've got to get back to work," Nina whispered, then turned toward him and beckoned. "Hi, Chief!"

Emily let out a tortured sigh. This was part of what she was afraid of. She adored her friends, but they were meddlesome at best, and the last thing she needed right now was to parade this fledgling friendship out in front of the two most observant people on the planet for them to dissect.

Greg gave Nina a strange look, then his gaze slid over to Emily again. She gave him a bashful shrug, and a smile toyed at the corners of his lips. He held up a finger to say he'd be a minute and turned back to the young man receiving take-out orders at the counter.

"Nina." Emily kept her voice low. "What are you doing?"

"Saying hello," she replied innocently. "Oh, don't worry about me. I'll be perfectly well behaved."

Greg gave the young man a smile and a nod, then turned back toward their booth. His thick, black police-issue shoes squeaked against the linoleum on his way over, and when he arrived at their booth, he leaned against the top of the seat next to Emily and looked down at them with an easy smile.

"Hi, ladies. Nice afternoon." His voice was deep and quiet. Emily looked up at him, the soft scent of his aftershave wafting down to her. His eyes met hers, and he gave her a slow smile. "How's Cora?"

"She's doing just fine." Emily glanced down at the baby. "Lunch break for you, too?"

"Yeah." He chuckled. "Best sub sandwiches here at Lou's."

"Oh, let me introduce my friends," Emily said. "This is Beth and Nina."

Beth smiled and reached out to shake his hand, as far as she could past her pregnant stomach. Nina did the same with a little more flexibility, and both women looked from Emily back to Greg in silence, their sparkling eyes saying more than enough.

"Nice to meet you," Greg said, seeming to ignore their silent exuberance and giving them each a polite nod. He looked down at Emily again and touched her shoulder. "Oh, Emily, are you free tomorrow night?"

"I think so." She looked back up at him to see something new in his eyes, something that looked almost like nerves.

"Say, around dinnertime?"

Emily laughed. "If you agree to feed me."

"Deal. Dinner it is. My place." He shot her a grin just as his phone rang on his hip. He looked down at the number and gave her an apologetic smile.

"Take it," she said. "I'll see you later."

As Greg moved away from the booth, his phone at his ear, Emily looked back to find Nina and Beth staring at her.

"What?" Emily asked.

"Just friends?" Beth asked, shaking her head.

"We were teasing you before," Nina confessed, "but, girl, there is something going on there."

"Like what?" Emily asked.

"Like dinner!" Beth retorted. "The man just asked you to dinner!"

"Well, yes, but…" Emily shrugged. "He's looking into my cousin's death."

"I don't even have the time to argue some sense into you," Nina said, opening her wallet and putting down some bills. "Lunch is on me, girls."

"Oh, you don't have to," Emily said.

"I insist." Nina shook her head. "Em, I was worried about you falling for him. I might need to worry about him falling for you."

Picking up his phone and moving away from the booth, Greg could feel Emily's friends' eyes on his back. He found it halfway amusing to cause a little stir, but more than that, he was downright relieved that she'd said yes to his dinner invitation. It would have been embarrassing to have her turn him down flat with witnesses.

"Chief Taylor here." He pinched his phone between his cheek and shoulder as he put some money on the counter and grabbed the to-go bags the server had left for him. "Thanks," he called to the server, then lowered his voice. "What can I do for you?"

"Hi, Chief, it's Benny."

"Do you have anything new?"

"I do. We found the victim's cell phone from that 11-80 a few weeks ago. It was jammed underneath a seat in the vehicle."

"Excellent." Greg pushed open the front door, the bell jingling over his head. He looked back in Emily's direction as he left, and she caught his eye with a small smile. He couldn't help the happiness that flooded through him at that look in her eyes, and he chuckled to himself.

"Is this really good news, Chief?" Benny asked.

FREE Merchandise is 'in the Cards' for you!

Dear Reader,

We're giving away FREE MERCHANDISE!

Seriously, we'd like to reward you for reading this novel by giving you **FREE MERCHANDISE** worth over $20. And no purchase is necessary!

You see the Jack of Hearts sticker above? Paste that sticker in the box on the Free Merchandise Voucher inside. Return the Voucher promptly...and we'll send you valuable Free Merchandise!

Thanks again for reading one of our novels—and enjoy your Free Merchandise with our compliments!

Pam Powers

Pam Powers

P.S. Look inside to see what Free Merchandise is **"in the cards"** for you!

HARLEQUIN® READER SERVICE—Here's How It Works:

Accepting your 2 free books and 2 free gifts (gifts valued at approximately $10.00) places you under no obligation to buy anything. You may keep the books and gifts and return the shipping statement marked "cancel." If you do not cancel, about a month later we'll send you 6 additional books and bill you just $4.74 each for the regular-print edition or $5.24 each for the larger-print edition in the U.S. or $5.24 each for the regular-print edition or $5.74 each for the larger-print edition in Canada. That is a savings of at least 21% off the cover price. It's quite a bargain! Shipping and handling is just 50¢ per book in the U.S. and 75¢ per book in Canada.* You may cancel at any time, but if you choose to continue, every month we'll send you 6 more books, which you may either purchase at the discount price or return to us and cancel your subscription.

*Terms and prices subject to change without notice. Prices do not include applicable taxes. Sales tax applicable in N.Y. Canadian residents will be charged applicable taxes. Offer not valid in Quebec. Books received may not be as shown. All orders subject to credit approval. Credit or debit balances in a customer's account(s) may be offset by any other outstanding balance owed by or to the customer. Please allow 4 to 6 weeks for delivery. Offer available while quantities last.

▲ If offer card is missing write to: Harlequin Reader Service, P.O. Box 1867, Buffalo, NY 14240-1867 or visit www.ReaderService.com ▲

BUSINESS REPLY MAIL
FIRST-CLASS MAIL   PERMIT NO. 717   BUFFALO, NY

POSTAGE WILL BE PAID BY ADDRESSEE

HARLEQUIN READER SERVICE
PO BOX 1867
BUFFALO NY 14240-9952

NO POSTAGE
NECESSARY
IF MAILED
IN THE
UNITED STATES

"No, no." Greg inwardly grimaced. "But it's definitely good news. Were you able to get any information off the phone?"

"Her call history was intact. It looks like there was one number she was communicating with more than any other."

"A boyfriend?" Greg asked. "Did you trace it?"

"Of course I traced it." Benny sounded mildly wounded. "And yes, the correspondent was male."

"Who was it?"

"You're going to love this, Chief. Things just got interesting."

"Who was it?" Greg repeated, slowly and succinctly. He was getting irritated.

"It's a private number with no voice mail."

"Hmm. That's suspicious."

"We'll need a warrant to get that information from the phone company."

"Definitely." Greg was good at this part. "I'm coming into the station. I'll make a few calls. We might be able to speed up the process a bit."

"That's what I thought." He could hear the grin in Benny's voice.

"Thanks, Benny. Good work."

As Greg snapped the phone shut, he looked back toward Lou's. He could see Emily's back in the window, and she had Cora in her arms, the tiny face peering over her shoulder. He sighed. This wasn't the first time that he felt tempted to have a family of his own, but it was the first time that the temptation was this strong.

Lord, give me strength.

He took a deep breath and pulled open his car door. He had an investigation under way.

Chapter Eleven

Greg liked open spaces. In fact, if he were to live in his dream home, it would be a log cabin in the Rockies, but that wasn't very realistic and he knew it. He was a cop first and foremost, and the cop in him won the debate every time. Log cabins in the middle of nowhere had to wait until he could take a few weeks off in a row for a vacation, and so far, that hadn't happened.

His house was a rustic little farmhouse on a three-acre lot just a few miles outside of Haggerston. The mountains loomed in the distance, a breathtaking view of white-crusted, jagged peaks out the west side of the house no matter the season. The farmhouse was small, with just a bedroom, small bathroom and kitchen. It had a broad veranda in the front and a little back door exiting off the kitchen in the back, heading out toward the old hand pump. Of course, he had running water and all the amenities, but he liked to use the old pump when he gardened. This little house was technically a historic site for Haggerston, and they probably would never have let him tear it down, even if he'd wanted to build something else. He hadn't even considered tearing it down, though. The hundred-year-old farmhouse suited him just fine.

The aroma of a beef roast broiling away in the oven mingled with the garlic mashed potatoes that Greg deposited on the table. He didn't cook a big meal often, but he was competent in the kitchen, and it felt good to have someone to eat with. Nate's Steak was a good place if he wanted company over a meal, but wings and fries were going to take a toll on the old ticker if he didn't watch it now.

The windows were all open, letting the heat of cooking out and a cool breeze in. Emily's car crunched down the drive, and he headed over to the front door. The late-afternoon light was golden and warm, spilling over the veranda in a familiar embrace. As Emily got out of the SUV, she waved at Greg with a brilliant smile. He couldn't help but admire her in the blue sundress she wore, long and flowing. She was a beautiful woman, and he found himself very aware of that fact. As she pulled Cora from the vehicle, she shot him another grin.

"Hi!" he called. "Did you find the place all right?"

"Oh, yes." She looked down at Cora and wiped a little dribble from the baby's chin. "You gave great directions."

"Sorry about the little show there in front of your friends." He felt the heat rising in his neck. "I probably shouldn't have done that. I wanted to give you some updates, and this seemed more comfortable than my office."

"Oh, no worries—they haven't had that much fun in ages." Emily laughed, hiking the baby bag higher on her slender shoulder.

Her hair hung loose down past her shoulders, swinging in a shimmering swath over the top of her back.

Stepping inside after her, he left the door open to keep the breeze moving.

"This place is amazing." Emily turned a full circle, looking over the refinished sitting room. He'd taken down the multiple layers of wallpaper, down to the boards. Then he'd whitewashed all of it, leaving more of a cottage feel to the place with a big circular rug in the center of the room. A potbellied stove stood prominently against the far wall, and a bookshelf held a collection of old family photos from group shots of generations past to a picture of his dad in police uniform, his mom smiling up at him adoringly. That was how he liked to remember them—still together.

"Thanks." Greg felt a bit of pride in his personal space. He wasn't one for a lot of visitors, tending to go out to socialize. "I wanted to keep it rustic."

"You're a log cabin kind of guy, aren't you?" she asked over her shoulder as she followed her nose toward the big, old stove.

"How did you know?"

"Oh, I'm not sure." She turned back again. "You just seem like the type to enjoy a sunrise and a faithful dog."

Greg chuckled. "Shotgun across my knee? Toothless?"

"Hiking boots. Cup of coffee." She gave him a cheerful smile, and he was surprised at how well she'd picked him. She'd actually described a perfect moment, truth be told.

"So what about you?" He chuckled. "Fifth Avenue? Swanky apartment?"

"Hardly!" She laughed. "I'd be your neighbor a few miles over. I'd really like to get far enough away from town to see the stars the way God intended."

"Really?" He eyed her with mild surprise.

"But not now." She looked over at Cora. "I have a little girl to raise alone, and I think I'd rather do that closer to family, if you know what I mean."

He nodded. He could understand that. Space was a great thing until you needed help, and then it was a curse. He liked the idea of having her live as close to him as possible, though.

"So what's cooking?" she asked.

"A roast and potatoes," he responded. "Nothing too fancy, but it was a chance to show off a bit." He smiled to himself at his little joke. "Actually, I have a bit of a lead on your cousin's case."

"What did you find?" She frowned and sank into a kitchen chair by the little table.

Greg grabbed a couple of plates from the cupboard and set about getting the rest of the meal on the table while he talked. "Well, first of all, we found your cousin's cell phone in the wreckage of the car, and her call history was still intact."

Emily was silent, her eyes pinned on him as he grabbed some oven mitts and pulled the big roasting tray out of the oven. The roast was nicely browned and sizzling. He stabbed it with a fork and pulled it out onto the cutting board to slice.

"There was one number that she communicated with more than others," he continued slowly. "So we focused on that one. It was a private number, and I had to go ahead and get a quick warrant from Judge Lincoln in order for the phone company to release any information to me, but once they did, I could see what all the secrecy was about."

"What was it?" Emily leaned down to take Cora out of her car seat.

"He's Charles Lindgren."

Emily sat back up, Cora looking surprised at the quick ride up, and Emily equally surprised at Greg's information. "Charles Lindgren? The senator?"

Greg nodded as he sliced the roast and laid the pieces on a plate. He paused in the task to look over at her. "But that isn't what I wanted to focus on."

"Okay…" Emily eyed him uncertainly, and he brought the plate of meat over to the table, along with a bowl of fresh greens. "So what's the important part here?"

"He's an older man with no children. His wife is younger than he is. If the money in your cousin's account came from him, it's possible that she was a surrogate mother for the couple."

"Do you think?" Emily frowned. "A baby surrogate… That sounds more like something people from Hollywood do."

"Or people with money. You have to be able to pay the young woman quite well to make it worth her while to carry another couple's pregnancy to term."

"If that were the case, she might have been running away with her baby, not wanting to give her up."

Greg nodded. "It's a possibility right now."

"What are the other ones?"

"The most obvious, I suppose." Greg sat down opposite Emily and sighed. "I know it might not be pleasant to hear, but it's quite possible that she had an illicit relationship with the senator."

Emily nodded slowly. "It does look that way, doesn't it?"

"I know that TV makes police work look so dramatic, but we generally find that if it walks like a duck and quacks like a duck…"

She nodded, not needing him to finish.

"But what I need from you is more of a gut reaction." Greg dished some potatoes and meat onto her plate, then served himself. "I'm just throwing out possibilities here, and you knew her."

Emily was silent for a long moment. "I have to say, being a politician's mistress? That doesn't sound like Jessica. She wasn't that type."

"What type was she?"

"The flower child. The free spirit."

"The surrogate mother?"

Emily shook her head. "I wish I knew."

"Senators don't set up private cell-phone numbers for no reason," Greg added. "And they don't have regular conversations with relatively poor artists for no reason, either. There was something to that relationship, and I want to find out what."

Emily looked over at Greg, fear flickering in her eyes. He was used to reading people's emotions in his line of work, and hers were coming across loud and clear. She was scared.

"Are you okay?" he asked, softening his tone.

"Is there someone else who's going to want her?" Emily asked, her voice trembling ever so slightly.

"Look, Emily…" Greg put down his fork, mentally chastising himself for being so stupid. "I'm just kind of brainstorming here. I'm really sorry. None of these things are proven. I'm just trying to figure out where to go with this. The senator is definitely a curiosity. I don't know what's happening yet. I shouldn't have said anything."

"No, no…" Emily reached across the table and gave his hand a quick squeeze in a spontaneously intimate gesture. "I'm no wilting flower over here. I asked you to look into it, and you warned me that I might find some things that I didn't want to know. So it serves me right."

His hand felt warm where she'd touched him, and he closed his fingers.

"Do you want me to stop?" Greg looked her in the eye, watching for signs of her true emotions on the matter, and when she shook her head in the negative, he believed her.

"No, this is better, actually. If I don't know, I'll always wonder and worry, waiting for the day someone shows up with more claim to her than I have. It's better to just face it, I think."

Greg liked her in that moment. It was more than attraction. It was more than interest. He saw strength, an ability to face life head-on, and he very sincerely liked Emily Shaw. He gave her a slow smile and nodded. "You've got grit."

"So what's the next step?" she asked.

"I look into this senator. I trace those big deposits in her checking account."

"It sounds like you know what you're doing." She looked down at Cora again, her eyes misting with sadness.

"Emily."

She looked up.

"I don't want you to worry about this. I'm still kicking myself for saying too much, but if there's one thing I've learned in my years as a cop, it's that the investigation isn't over till the fat lady sings."

"And who's the fat lady here?" Emily asked, humor shining past the sadness.

"I think the fat lady is the senator this time around. It doesn't make sense right now because we don't have all the pieces to the puzzle. When we do, it'll make perfect sense. Until then, nothing is answered, okay?"

"Okay." She nodded and straightened her spine. "You're right."

They focused on eating after that, and after they had finished much of the meal, Greg looked down at Cora. Emily had pulled out a bottle, and she was drinking hungrily, her eyes drooping in fatigue.

"So..." He lifted his eyes to meet Emily's thoughtful gaze and blurted out matter-of-factly, "I made dessert."

"Oh?" Emily's eyes lit up. "Greg, you can really cook. I'm impressed. So what's for dessert?"

Greg pushed himself back from the table and headed to the fridge. Waiting in two soup bowls that did nothing for presentation was the chocolate mousse he'd whipped up the night before. He figured he'd inflicted enough damage for one day, and it was time to start soothing the wounds with chocolate.

He remembered being a small boy and watching his father make chocolate mousse. His big, muscular dad would stand there with the mixer, whipping up the fluffy mounds of chocolate.

"Do you know why I'm making mousse, son?" he'd asked.

"Why?"

"Because your mother loves it. One day you'll get married, too."

"Will I have to make mousse?"

"If you know what's good for you!" Then his dad would throw back his head and belt out his hearty laugh. "I'll show you how. Don't you worry."

Then Greg would get to lick the beaters, which had always been his favorite part.

His dad never had shown Greg how to make chocolate mousse. He'd died before that little father-son moment came their way, so one day, on the anniversary of his father's death, Greg had gone online, found some chocolate-mousse recipes and put himself to work. He'd never had the "guy talk" with his father. He'd never been advised on how to deal with his first date or his first kiss. He'd never been told how to be a good husband or how to deal with women, besides the little secret of chocolate mousse. So learning how to make the dessert had become a way to connect with his dad long-distance, so to speak.

Coming back to the table with a dish of chocolate mousse in each hand, he couldn't help the smile that played at the corners of his lips as he saw Emily's eyes light up.

"Greg, you never cease to surprise me." She looked up at him, impressed. "This looks amazing."

Settling down at the table again, he looked across at the beautiful woman, infant in arms, who sat at his kitchen table. He didn't know what the future held for them, but he had a pretty good idea that if he'd had the chance to ask his dad's advice on what he was supposed to do with a woman this beautiful and a situation this complicated, he would have said, "Chocolate mousse, Greg. Chocolate mousse."

That evening, stuffed from a spectacular dinner of roast beef and the creamiest chocolate mousse to ever pass her lips, Emily sat in her living room, Cora cuddled up against her chest. Crickets chirped somewhere outside the window, lulling her anxiety. It was a gorgeous night, the kind where the scent of flowers floated on a warm breeze and the stars glittered like diamonds. Up above the world so high, like a diamond in the sky. Emily turned her head as far as she could to look up through the window. She could just see a wedge of black velvet sky before turning back to face the room.

Cora's little head had that sweet baby scent, and Emily closed her eyes for a long moment, inhaling that smell she loved so much, memorizing it.

Lord, will she be mine? Is this the beginning of a life-time together, or is there a father out there with greater rights to her than any of us?

The visit with Greg had conjured up the very real possibility of finding Cora's biological father. Why wasn't he in Jessica's life? Or had he been in Jessica's life against her will? It was hard to know, but the thought that a man out there might be able to walk in and de-mand his daughter be returned to him was a scary one.

Cora let out a deep sigh in her sleep and Emily looked down at her, at those fine little eyelashes and the wisps of orange-blond hair that stood up straight from her head like the plumes of a bird. Emily lifted one tiny hand up to her lips and gave her a light kiss.

Other nights, Emily would have slipped Cora into bed by this time, but tonight was different. Tonight, she didn't want to put her down.

A few months earlier, Beth had squealed out her news that she was pregnant. It had been barely a year after Emily's hysterectomy, and the news had stung. She'd smiled as brightly as possible, told Beth how thrilled she was for the news and then gone home and cried.

It wasn't that Beth hadn't had her own fertility strug-gles. She and Howard had tried to conceive for years with no success, and then one day, after months of look-ing into adoption, Beth was suddenly pregnant. Beth de-served this. She deserved to have a baby and to be happy with her adoring husband. She deserved all of it, but that didn't make the sting any less for Emily.

She had no husband and no chance of having children of her own. While she hated giving herself a pity party, she'd eventually got over it and given the pain over to God. God was the one with plans, and she was the one who would just have to wait.

Now, with a baby in her arms before Beth had even given birth, she'd felt blessed. God hadn't forgotten her. Yet was this part of God's plan for her, after all? Or was it just a red herring, something tossed at her that got her hopes up and steered her into a new and unexpected direction?

An image of Greg rose up in her mind at that thought… the handsome chief of police with those gentle blue eyes and strong, broad shoulders. He was something unexpected, that man. If only he wanted to have children, too. Would it be so terrible to end up married to a sweet guy like Greg? Would it be enough?

Looking down at the baby asleep on her chest, Emily sighed. *Can I have both, Lord?* She was half joking, because she knew that wasn't possible. So instead, she sang softly to Cora, "Twinkle, twinkle, little star, how I wonder what you are…."

The song was still comforting, even after all these years, and she remembered the safe feeling of her father singing over her in her bed at night. There was a verse in the Bible that talked about that—a verse she'd memorized years ago: *The LORD your God is with you, the Mighty Warrior who saves. He will take great delight in you; in His love He…will rejoice over you with singing.*

She felt a flood of peace, and she sighed. She could feel God close to her there in the quiet summer night, and for the first time since Cora had come home to her, Emily let the tears come. Sometimes a girl just needed to cry it out and let her Father comfort her.

Chapter Twelve

The next afternoon, as she drove toward the one shopping mall that Haggerston had to offer, Emily felt drained, both from the emotional turmoil lately and from the heat. South Haggerston Mall, which vainly suggested the possibility of more malls in the town, was a small building with about fourteen stores in total, most of which catered to elderly people's fashion. The "food court," if it could even be called such a thing, consisted of two restaurants. This was the best that Haggerston had to offer in a mall setting. The rest of the Haggerston shopping experience was street side in a lovely downtown with hanging planters and stores that kept their doors propped open in hopes of getting an errant breeze. Emily wasn't interested in the shopping, though. She was interested in the air-conditioning, so the mall was her destination.

The heat shimmered off the road in mirages as she drove along. Summer, it seemed, had kicked it into high gear. Emily kept her windows up and the air-conditioning blasting, enjoying the brief relief. She'd get used to the heat soon enough, but the first few days were hard, and she was worried that they'd be harder still on tiny Cora.

Glancing in her rearview mirror, she saw the same nondescript sedan behind her still. That was odd. How many people could be taking her route for this long? She shrugged it off. It was a small place, and there was only one downtown. She signaled for a turn, eyeing the car behind her again. It slowed, but didn't signal. As she turned onto a side road, the car didn't follow, but when she looked again, she saw it stopped at the corner. After a good distance was between them, it eased around and started after her again.

Am I being followed?

It was almost a ridiculous question to ask herself, because this was Haggerston, after all. Nothing happened here, and life wasn't a TV show. *That's it. I watch too much TV,* she decided firmly. She signaled again onto Sherwood Drive. This was the long way to the mall, but she was curious to see what would happen.

A few moments later, the car eased around the corner and slowed to put more space between them. Her heart sped up. This might be Haggerston, but she was definitely being followed. She took a sharp turn into the mall parking lot and found a space near the doors. She sat there, scanning the parking-lot entrance.

Nothing. The car didn't turn in.

Her heart began to slow down its galloping pace, and she let out a nervous laugh.

"It looks like I'm just paranoid." She chuckled aloud. "Well, Cora, let's go wander around the mall." She sounded more convincing than she felt, and that was a good thing. Cora needed a calm and reassuring mother, not someone panicking over a drive to the mall.

Emily took one last look around the parking lot, but still saw nothing, so she exited the vehicle and got the baby ready to go into the mall. She made the quick trip to the front doors, and as she stepped inside the mall she let out a shiver. The air-conditioning felt wonderful, but her attention was behind her. Where was that car?

She stood at the door for a moment, watching, but didn't see anything. *Paranoid. That's it.* She took a deep breath, willing herself to relax.

"All right, Cora. Now it's time for us to just cool off." Emily looked at the baby up on her shoulder, her big blue eyes taking in the colors and lights around them. "It isn't much, sweetie," Emily crooned. "But it's air-conditioned, and that'll have to do."

As she walked around up and down the one corridor that made up the South Haggerston Mall, she tried to calm her nerves with silent prayer. God was in control, and she really had to stop this irrational panicking. Was this the kind of thing mothers felt with their keen need to protect their babies, or was this something more?

She stopped to look at a rack of sale tops, all of which looked more suited to a woman in her sixties than someone her age. She flicked through the assorted colors and nodded at the shopkeeper, a woman in her forties with a hairdo about a decade too old for her.

"They're all half off," she called from her perch on a stool. "I have other sizes inside, too, if you need more options."

"Thanks." Emily tried to look as noncommittal as possible and continued wandering down the way. The shoe shop had a rack of laces on display, and the bookstore ahead seemed to be the most promising time waster for the day. Emily picked up her pace, but glancing back, she saw a young man talking to the saleswoman where she'd stopped. He wore a pair of jeans and a button-up shirt. His haircut was more expensive than Haggerston had to offer. Emily ducked into the bookshop, then looked back out. The man was gone.

Pull yourself together, Em. What's wrong with you?

The front of the store had a display of biographies, and Emily picked up one about the Queen of England. She would have flipped through the glossy pictures in the center if she'd had both hands free, but carrying a baby and doing anything else seemed to be more difficult than she'd imagined.

"Jessica?"

Emily stiffened at the deep voice, and she froze. That was her cousin's name.

"Jessica?" The voice was low and now just over her shoulder. She whirled around to see the man she'd seen talking to the shopkeeper a moment ago looking at her pointedly over his sunglasses, his gaze steely and direct. The muscles in his jaw tensed, and he stood stock-still as if ready to pounce.

"Who?" Emily asked, her voice foreign in her own ears.

His eyes moved down to Cora, and Emily took a step back, turning sideways so that Cora was as far from him as possible. His eyes moved over Cora slowly and methodically, then turned back to Emily.

"I don't know you!" Emily said loudly. "Who are you?"

"You okay, Ms. Shaw?" the saleswoman called from the cash register.

"No!" she called back. "This man is harassing me. Call security."

He took a step backward, but not an alarmed step. He'd heard what the saleswoman had called her, too, and he'd registered it. He was neither alarmed nor intimidated.

"Sorry for the confusion," he said smoothly, moving away from her again. "My mistake."

As he disappeared outside the store again, Emily stood there beside the pile of biographies, her knees trembling. That was the man who had been following her, she was willing to guess. He was looking for Jessica...and Cora.

Emily pulled her cell phone out of her purse and dialed Greg's number.

"Are you all right?" the saleswoman asked, coming around the counter. Emily knew her. She was the mother of one of her students from a couple of years earlier. "Should I call the police?"

"I'm doing that now." Emily's mouth was dry, and she shook off the woman's attempt to lead her to a chair. She wanted to keep her eyes peeled in case that man returned, and she wasn't about to be shushed and patted as if she were hysterical.

"Hello?" Greg's voice sounded distracted, and she could hear hubbub in the background. "No, file that one. I need two of these, though."

"Greg, something just happened." Even now, it felt as if the events were unraveling in her mind.

"Emily? Are you okay?"

"I'm fine, but there was this man. He just came and..." It had all seemed so coherent and complete a moment ago, and now she wasn't sure how to explain it. "He called me Jessica."

She closed her eyes for a moment, frustrated. That wasn't proof of anything. This wasn't coming out right.

"What are you talking about?" The voices and noise from the background got quieter, and Greg's voice was low and reassuring in her ear. "Are you sure you're okay?"

"I don't know. This man... I think I was followed here. Then I saw him talking to the lady I was just talking to. Then he came right up behind me and called me Jessica and looked at Cora like a—like a snake about to swallow her."

"I'm on my way. Where are you?"

"At the mall."

"I'll be there in ten minutes. Stay where you are."

Emily stood there for a moment, holding her phone. Was she being paranoid? She tried to focus on the events as they'd happened; it all seemed so flimsy and ridiculous when she tried to put it into words, but she felt something heavy and filled with foreboding in her stomach. That man had followed her, and he was convinced she must be Jessica. What had Jessica been involved in?

"Did you want to sit down, miss?" the saleslady asked. "You look kind of spooked. Who was that guy? Some old boyfriend?"

"No." Emily tried to push down her irritation. "He's not some old boyfriend. I don't know him."

"He sure seemed to know you."

Emily nodded silently. Yes, he did. Except for her first name.

"Not bad-looking, though." The woman laughed self-consciously. "Wonder if he's single..."

Emily clenched her teeth together. *Because that's the important thing here, whether or not the creepy stalker is married.* She resisted the urge to roll her eyes.

"I'm waiting for the police. They'll be here in ten minutes," she said instead. "Maybe you could remember what he looked like to give them a description."

The woman looked slightly miffed and she moved away, but this was probably the most excitement she'd seen all month, so she hovered around the store entrance, looking for signs of the promised police.

The minutes ticked slowly by, but when Greg strolled up, another officer in tow, looking into each store, Emily let out a sigh of relief. He stood in the entrance, his ice-blue eyes sweeping the shop, lingering on her for a brief moment then darting back out into the mall. After a thorough scan, he stepped inside.

"Are you all right?" Greg stood there with his police hat on his head and the heel of his hand resting casually on his gun, but when he came toward her, he relaxed and reached out, giving her arm a reassuring squeeze.

"There was a man bothering her," the saleswoman said excitedly. "He's gone now, but he wanted to talk to her or something."

The look on Greg's face told Emily that the woman wasn't entirely helpful. "What happened?" He turned toward Emily.

"He was kind of good-looking," the saleswoman went on. "Like this tall, nice shoulders..."

"Thanks." Greg gave her a cool smile. "I just want to ask Ms. Shaw here what happened, and that officer over there is going to get your statement, okay?"

"Suit yourself." The woman shrugged, but lingered close by.

"Let's walk," Greg said in a low voice. He took her arm in his warm grip and steered her out of the store. "Now, I need you to slow it down and explain to me what happened."

Emily put together the details as best she could, but even as she talked, she realized that the few flimsy events were tied together by her own feelings, nothing more. When she was finished, Greg nodded slowly.

"Do I sound paranoid?" Emily asked warily. "Hearing myself say it out loud, I sound nuts."

"No, you don't sound paranoid at all. You sound like you were followed."

Emily wasn't sure if she felt relieved to hear that or not. She gave him a wry smile. "I think I might like being nuts better."

Greg chuckled, then turned serious again. "Look, something weird happened here, and you aren't the paranoid type. From what I can see, someone is looking for Jessica and doesn't know that she's dead."

"And Cora?"

"Obviously they were looking for a young woman with an infant. Here's hoping Cora isn't the goal."

Emily felt a twinge of fear work its way up her spine. She took a deep, wavery breath. "Who would do this?"

"I don't know. Do you?" He looked at her directly, his eyes watching her carefully.

She shook her head, then she frowned. "Maybe Steve knows more than he's letting on."

Greg nodded. "It's occurred to me, too."

Cora's eyes were closed now, her head resting against Emily's neck. Her arm ached from the position it was in, and Emily let out a sigh. "I'm so tired."

"I'll follow you home, and we'll put a couple of cruisers on your house for the next little while. If this guy comes around again, he'll see police presence."

"Thanks." She adjusted the sleeping Cora in her arms. "I appreciate it."

As Greg steered her toward the outside door, she could feel his alertness, even in the gentle pressure of his fingertips on her elbow. He was still looking for something, for some clue to what was happening, and that was a relief. She wasn't on her own here. Thank goodness, Greg didn't think she was crazy.

"I'd feel better if I could keep a personal eye on you tomorrow," Greg said as they stepped out into the bright sunlight.

"What did you have in mind?" She looked over at him, feeling a smile come to her lips.

"Come to church with me," he offered. "It'll take the pressure off you for a day, and I'll feel better having you within sight."

"Actually, that might be nice," she admitted. Just for one day, to let someone else do the worrying about people following her sounded like the break she needed.

"Good." His blue eyes softened, and he shot her a grin. "You'll be okay. Trust me. No one is getting past me, all right?"

She nodded and returned his smile. Somehow, that made her feel a lot better.

That evening, after Cora was in bed, Emily's fear turned to anger. Someone was following her, and she knew of one person who had an interest in scaring her—Steve. Pacing her kitchen floor for a few minutes, she tried to piece it all together again in her mind. It still didn't make sense. If Steve knew something, maybe this would make him spill it.

Dialing his number, she took a deep breath, willing herself to calm down.

"Hello, Shaw residence." It was Sara. Just great. Emily was probably the last person Sara wanted to chat with, and she knew it. Emily sighed.

"Hi, Sara, how are you?"

"Emily?"

"Yes, it's me. How are you doing?"

"We're all fine. We're just having family worship."

"Oh, I'm sorry to interrupt. I can call back later."

There was some muffled talking on the other end of the line, and then Sara said sweetly, "No, no, Steve is right here. I'll continue with the children."

There was something so irritating about Sara's carefully controlled sweetness. She said things like "the Lord willing" and "the children" in a breathy voice that sounded more like bad acting than anything else. Now was not the time to quibble, though, so Emily said a quick "Thanks, Sara" and listened while the phone was passed over.

"Emily?" Steve sounded eager. "Hi."

"Hi, Steve." Emily felt suddenly tired. "I had a bit of a...I guess a scare today. Someone followed me."

"What?" He didn't sound as if he believed her. "Are you sure? Should I come get Cora?"

"Yes, I'm sure, and no, you shouldn't." She sighed. This wasn't going to be a pleasant chat, she could already tell.

"You're under a lot of stress," Steve said. "Maybe a few days off from taking care of her would help."

"Steve, I'm not paranoid. I was followed."

"How do you know?"

"The police believed me, for one," she said. "And the guy called me Jessica."

There was silence on the other end. "But she's dead."

"I realize that. Hence it being really, really creepy." Emily couldn't help the irritation from entering her voice. "Sorry. I know that was a bit of a shock. It upset me, too. Look, some guy followed me from my home to the mall and confronted me there. He thought I was Jessica, that much was obvious."

"Why? What did he want?"

"Beats me. I was hoping you knew something."

"Like what?"

"Like who this creep is! Do you know anything from Jessica's life that might explain this? I look nothing like her, but..."

"The baby." His voice was low.

"It occurred to me. So what do you know?"

Steve was silent again. Emily could hear some little voices singing "Jesus Loves Me" in the background.

"Steve?"

"Emily, it sounds to me like Cora is in danger. Let me come get her."

"I have police protection, Steve. This guy isn't going to get to me again. Besides, there's something you haven't considered yet."

"What's that?"

"Cora has a father, Steve. And whoever that father is has a bigger claim to Cora than either of us."

There was silence on the other end again, and Emily could hear Sara's voice reading a Bible story.

"Well." Steve sighed. "It doesn't change anything right now, does it?"

"For Cora's safety," Emily said on a sigh, "call Greg at the station if you remember anything."

"Greg? You're on a first-name basis with the chief of police now?"

So are you, Steve, she thought to herself in irritation, but arguing about this wasn't going to help anything tonight.

"Can't we work together to figure this out?" Emily asked, exasperated.

"Of course. I'll call if I can think of anything."

As Emily hung up the phone, she deeply doubted her cousin's good intentions. Her lawyer would be very irritated with her for this call, she knew already, but at least she'd given it a shot. They were supposed to be a family, after all, and if at the end of all of this Cora didn't have a family left to rely on, she would have lost more than she'd ever know.

Chapter Thirteen

Sunday dawned bright and sunny, the kind of summer day where it felt impossible to complain. As Emily buckled Cora into her car seat in the back of Greg's car, she smiled to herself. Cora was about as cute as she could get in her little green sundress with a matching green headband. She wore the tiniest white sandals that Emily had been able to find, although they were still a little big, and Emily felt a swell of pride.

"You look really nice."

Emily glanced up at Greg, who stood by the open driver's-side door, leaning against the roof. He was dressed casually in gray dress pants and a white linen button-up shirt, open at the neck. A gun holster came over his shoulders, and he eased a sport coat over the weapon. He gave her a smile, and she squinted at him quizzically.

"Do you need to be armed?"

"I'm a cop, Emily." He met her gaze evenly. "I'm here to protect you today. I won't pull out my gun unless absolutely necessary, but I need to be prepared, okay?"

She nodded.

"You look nice, by the way," he said.

"Thanks." She'd worn the most conservative sundress she owned, a navy ship-christening's dress with an A-line skirt and double-breasted buttons running down the front. She'd left her glossy hair down, and she tucked it behind her ear as she looked up at him. "Beth would be proud. She's always trying to get me to visit other churches."

"Why?"

"To meet eligible men." Emily rolled her eyes.

Greg laughed. "You don't strike me as the type to be easily pawned off on some unsuspecting guy."

"Thanks." She paused. "I think."

"It's a compliment." He smiled at her, his blue eyes meeting hers, making the heat rise in her cheeks.

Instead of answering him, she slid into the front seat of the car. As Greg settled in the driver's seat next to her, she could smell the subtle scent of his cologne. She sank back in the seat, enjoying the convenience of being driven somewhere instead of doing the driving. Greg put his arm around the back of her seat as he backed out of her drive, and as he pulled it back to shift into first, his eye caught her watching him.

"How are you feeling since the stalker?" he asked.

"I'm installing a security system."

He laughed softly. "Good plan. In a place like Hagger ston, we don't like to think we need that kind of thing, but the truth is, we're sitting ducks to every passing criminal if we aren't ready."

Emily nodded, her mind moving back to her cousins. "Some things you don't want to see. The truth can be hard to take, especially in your own family."

"Are you talking about Steve?"

"He's my cousin. I grew up with him. He drove me nuts, yes, but he's...he's Steve. I'm seeing this whole new side to him now, and I hate that. I just don't want to see it."

Greg was silent, a frown puckering his brow. After a few moments, he said, "I gave him a call last night."

"Me, too," she admitted.

Greg looked over at her, eyebrows raised in surprise. "Oh?"

"I got absolutely nothing out of him. And for that pleasure, my lawyer is going to be furious with me."

He chuckled. "That he will."

"Did you find out anything?"

"Nothing directly, no."

"Anything indirectly?"

"Just a few suspicions."

Emily nodded. He didn't seem willing to open up any more than that, and she could respect it. He was a police officer, and she didn't really expect him to tell her every detail. Instead, she looked out the window at the passing fields of yellow canola and the looping telephone wires as they headed toward town.

"Nervous?" he asked.

"About what?" She looked back at him.

"Coming to church with me."

"A bit." She returned his grin.

"Don't worry—I'm the one who should be worried."

"Why?"

"I'm about to walk into my home church with a beautiful woman and a new baby." He gave her a comically arch expression. "Tongues will wag, my dear."

Emily blushed and laughed. "Well, I can't help that. You brought this on yourself."

"Yeah, I did," he replied. "This Sunday dinner will be the most exciting one they'll have had in a while."

"For the gossip?"

"Gossip is always better before you know the truth." His gaze softened as he looked at her. "Besides, it's worth it."

Emily looked over at him, feeling suddenly shy. The thought that Greg would brave the gossip and curiosity in order to keep an eye on her was strangely touching.

"You've never brought a woman to church with you before, have you?" Emily asked.

"Does my mom count?"

Emily rolled her eyes and laughed out loud. "Oh, Greg, they're going to eat you alive!"

"You're probably right." He chuckled. "But most of that will happen behind my back, and the rest of it will wait until they run into me in town."

Small towns had that way about them. Everybody was somehow connected to everyone else, and gossip flew around town faster than a stomach bug.

"You're a lot shyer than you let on, aren't you?" she asked.

"I prefer to call it *private*." He gave her a wink. "It's manlier that way."

He pulled onto a tree-lined street with a white steepled church farther up the road. It was beautiful, the white of the old-fashioned church peeking through the lush green of the summer leaves. He pulled into a parking spot along the side of the road and turned off the car. He looked over at her, his blue eyes meeting hers for a moment, a smile twitching at the corners of his lips.

"Well," he said. "Shall we go in?"

As they walked up toward the church, Greg glanced over his shoulder, scanning the familiar street for anyone who might be following. Nothing that he could see, but blending into a street already lined with parked cars would be an easy enough feat. One of the cruisers slowed down as it passed the church, and he nodded to the officer in the vehicle.

Emily carried the car seat in one hand, and he carried the diaper bag over his shoulder. He knew exactly how they looked, and he liked it. If anyone were following Emily, he wanted them to see her with a protector— even better if they knew him as chief of police. Emily was not alone in this, and that was the message he was sending loud and clear.

Emily's dark hair framed her face, and her calf-length sailor dress swirled around her calves like a forties movie star. She wore a simple black pair of heels, and he liked the sound they made against the sidewalk. She glanced up at him and gave him a shy smile.

As they came up the walk, Greg could already hear the piano music pounding out traditional hymns, and he felt that familiar wave of peace come over him. Church was a place where he could step away from his job and his obligations and just give it up to God. Of course, God was with him through the week, as well, but there was something comforting about Sunday, a day where he gave himself permission to step away. He took a deep breath and let it out, then glanced down at Emily at his side. She was comfortably petite next to him, and he found himself wanting to put his arm around her and pull her close, but he didn't dare.

"Good morning, Chief." The reverend was a slender, older man with white hair and a ready smile. He shook Greg's hand and turned his attention to Emily.

"This is Emily Shaw." Greg felt a bit of pride at introducing her.

"Ms. Shaw, this is a pleasure," the reverend said, taking her hand. "I'm glad to have you with us today. And who is this?"

Greg saw a sudden look of uncertainty flash over Emily's face, and he had the urge to rescue her from the moment, but she recovered quickly and flashed a brilliant smile.

"This is Cora."

"She's lovely." The reverend's glance swept over them together. "You make a beautiful family."

Greg had known the reverend for several years, and the old reverend knew Greg's personal situation quite well. He chuckled to himself.

Nothing like a little pastoral nudge in the matrimonial direction.

He swallowed his laugh, but he met the reverend's eyes with humor as they walked past. A beautiful family. Yes, they did look good together, and he did like this feeling of having them with him. If he were the parenting sort, he could see himself referring to them as his two favorite girls...but there was no point in letting his mind run that course.

The foyer of the church was dim due to the old-fashioned architecture. This building had been a place of worship for the past seventy-five years at least. The swinging doors that led to the sanctuary were a heavy, polished walnut, and as Greg pushed a door open for Emily to walk through, he felt a mixture of peace and uncertain happiness.

They'd all ask about her next week, he knew. And what would he say? That she was a friend? That this was about a case and nothing else? They would nod and make that good-humored face that said they knew exactly what kind of friend she was, and they thought it was high time for that sort of addition to his life. They'd ask for details. They'd bring her up for weeks to come. There would be no forgetting about this Sunday and packing it away into another box in his mind. That was the part that made him nervous. He was crossing a line here, allowing her into his personal life, and he knew that this would have ripples.

They slid into a pew toward the back, just in case Emily needed to take Cora out to settle her, and as they sat down, the piano struck up the chords for "In the Sweet By and By." The old piano, just slightly out of tune, plunked away as the voices of the congregation joined together in the familiar hymn. An old lady's voice wavered in a shrill soprano near the front, just half a beat behind everyone else. The man leading the congregation up front was conducting in the air with a great amount of enthusiasm, and Greg let his eyes flow over everyone, scouting for someone who didn't belong. This was part of why he'd suggested she come to his church.

In one of the pews ahead of them, Richard Pike sat with his teenage son.

Funny how life turns out.

Richard had been the one to break Greg's nose in the fifth grade. He'd returned the favor at the end of the school year, but that school year had been hell. It was years ago, and Richard was no longer a bullying brute of a kid. He was now the divorced dad of a teenage boy who was slender and quiet—the perfect target for the current bullies at the local high school. Greg had taken some time with the boy, talking to him about the bullying.

"I appreciate this, Greg," Richard had said in a private conversation. "Vince is sensitive, and it means a lot that you'd take him under your wing a bit. I'm not so good with the...with the feelings and all that. After how I treated you, I—" He'd cleared his throat. "Appreciate it, man."

It was as close to an apology as Greg would ever get.

Cora made a little mewling sound, and he glanced over to see Emily gently taking her out of the car seat and settling her into her lap. They were a beautiful pair, these two, and he felt his heart soften just looking at them. She glanced up at him then leaned close, her faint perfume tickling his nose.

"Could you get the bottle, Greg?"

He pulled himself together and opened the diaper bag, entirely uncertain of what he'd find there. There were the expected diapers, some cloths, a few jars of ointments and creams, a couple changes of clothes for Cora and several bottles. He pulled one out and handed it to Emily, who popped the lid off with one flick of her finger and popped the nipple into Cora's hungry little mouth.

Emily cradled Cora, who slurped the bottle hungrily, in the crook of her arm. Emily looked so alone just then, cuddling the baby and sitting on the pew in perfect silence and solitude. She had an air about her that could make her seem as if she was a million miles away, all on her own like a star in the sky. But he didn't think she wanted to be so alone....

Before he had the time to think better of it, Greg slid his arm around her shoulder and nudged her closer to him. She leaned toward him in response, and he could feel the warmth of her arm against his side. He suddenly felt a wave of nervousness, like a teenage boy making his first move, and he looked down at her, wondering what she was thinking.

It felt good to hold her like this. It felt right, somehow, as if this was exactly where they belonged, side by side. He ran his hand down her bare arm and felt goose bumps. She was cold.

Cora started to fuss a little, and Emily made some soft shushing noises, patting her little bottom with one hand. Looking down at them, Greg suddenly felt entirely helpless to keep himself aloof. He shouldn't be falling for her, but he was.

"Greg?" she whispered.

He leaned down to catch her words.

"I think I'd better change her...."

And just like that, Emily was out of his arms again, her heels clicking softly against the wooden floor as she disappeared out the back door, Cora in her arms and the diaper bag over her shoulder. The only thing left behind was the car seat, sitting at his feet.

So this was what a family felt like. It wasn't quite what he'd imagined, but he'd never really allowed himself to imagine these sorts of things before. And now that he sat here in his church, the old reverend standing up to preach and his side still warm with the feeling of her arm, he felt his firm resolve wavering.

Father God, I didn't want to know what this felt like. I didn't want to know what I was missing.

For the first time ever, he felt a wave of desperate longing for the exact thing that he could not have. It was this—this right here. He wanted to do this every Sunday for the rest of his life, and he had a feeling that he'd never be able to sit in a pew again with the same sense of peace he'd had up to this point.

He knew exactly what he was missing.

Pushing himself to his feet, he discreetly followed in the direction she'd gone. She could competently change a diaper without his help, but he was definitely going to keep an eye on her. With some unknown man following her and too many unanswered questions for his liking, he'd feel better when this case was resolved. Then he could settle back into his routine and talk himself out of whatever it was he was feeling for her.

That afternoon, Emily and Greg ambled down a gravel side road by Emily's house. Cora was cuddled into a snuggly on Emily's chest, a warm breeze ruffling her downy hair. It felt comfortable walking this way, Cora in her arms and Greg by her side. Big, fluffy clouds tumbled across the blue sky, their shadows following them across the vast fields.

"Who was that young man you were talking to after church?" Emily asked.

"That was Vincent Pike. He's Richard Pike's son."

"Richard Pike, the football star who made you miserable in grade school?" she asked.

"The one and only." One side of Greg's mouth twitched upward in a wry smile. "His son is a good kid, but he's been bullied a lot in school."

"Oh…" Emily let her gaze wander over the fields, young wheat waving green and verdant over the gently rolling countryside. The mountains in the distance glistened with white, a silent reminder of the cool weather ahead. "That's ironic, isn't it? The bully's son getting bullied?"

"It is. It's also really sad. Richard had no idea how to help his son through this. For the first year that it happened, Richard just told him to suck it up." Greg frowned. "It wasn't that Richard didn't care. He just didn't know how to help. He thought toughening Vincent up would fix things."

"That's what my uncle Hank did to Jessica. Not

toughening her up, exactly, but getting quite tough on her, trying to straighten her out. It backfired."

Greg nodded. "I'm not a dad, but from what I've seen in my line of work, it isn't a tough parent that gets results. It's a relationship."

"How is Vincent doing now?"

"He's doing really well. He found a group of kids he gets along with, and there is always safety in numbers, it seems. Richard asked if I'd—" he paused, shrugged "—mentor Vincent. I guess that's the word."

"Hang out with him a bit and help him figure things out?"

Greg grinned. "Something like that. He's a good kid—smart, creative. All he needed was a group of kids who were like him, and he was able to really take off. I may have also shown him a couple little tricks to get a guy off his back."

Emily chuckled. "You taught him how to apprehend a suspect, didn't you?"

Greg laughed out loud. "I'm not admitting to anything. He now knows how to deal with a bigger assailant without hurting him...too badly."

"Vincent is lucky to have you." Emily nodded, impressed. "Richard, too, for that matter. Was it hard to forgive him?"

"It was a long time ago." Greg shook his head. "I think being a Christian made it easier for me to let go of that, as well."

"I could see that," Emily said softly.

They slowed to a stop, and Emily inhaled the summer scent of dusty roads and fresh wind.

"I'm sure your faith has changed your outlook, too."

"Absolutely." Emily patted Cora's back when she squirmed. "God gives strength, but I also think my faith keeps my perspective fresh. Every child is a child of God. There are no losers. There are no wastes."

"Amen to that. I'm willing to guess that in a few years, you'll have some kids coming back to tell you that you made all the difference in their lives."

Emily blushed. "I don't need to be all the difference, but a small difference would be gratifying."

Greg angled his head in the direction they had come. "Ready to head back?"

"I think so. Cora will be ready for a bottle soon."

The gravel road crunched under their shoes, and she smiled up at Greg. "This feels more like a fun day together than a security escort."

"Does it?" He chuckled. "Well, this has to be the most enjoyable police escort I've ever done."

His steel-blue eyes scanned the road, then his gaze swung around them.

"Do you see anyone?" she asked.

He shook his head. "Don't worry too much. No one is getting to you on my watch."

His tone was low and gravelly, and when she looked over at him, his jaw was tensed and his gaze sharp. Just as she looked away from the road, her foot went into a dip and her knee buckled.

Greg's arm shot out and he caught her, easily lifting her back to her feet with his strong grip.

"Whoa, you okay?" he asked, his arm staying around her waist as she steadied herself. Turning toward him, she found that direct, steely gaze locked on hers and she caught her breath. His eyes moved slowly over her face, and a smile tickled the corners of his lips.

"I'm—" She swallowed, forgetting what she had started to say.

Greg gently pulled a wisp of hair out of her eyes, then

dropped his hand from her waist. He didn't say anything, but as they continued walking, he scooped her hand up into his. His warm, strong fingers wrapped comfortably around hers, and she resisted the urge to lean into that hard, muscled arm.

As they walked along, the wind sweeping over the rippling fields of young wheat, Emily settled into his pace, enjoying the companionable silence. He was so strong, so sure of himself, that she almost felt as if he swept her along with him in his slow, powerful stride. A hawk peered down at them from its perch atop a power pole, but she didn't bother pointing it out. The silence was perfect, comfortable, and she didn't want to shatter the moment and have him let go.

The mile flew by, and when they approached her house, he gave her hand a gentle squeeze, then released her.

"Did you want to come in?" she asked softly.

Greg looked down into her eyes, then slowly shook his head. "I'd better not."

"You sure?"

He laughed softly. "No, I'm doing my best to keep things—" he shot her a bashful grin "—professional."

Emily shrugged her shoulders and smiled back. "Thought I'd ask."

"I've got a patrol car keeping a pretty close eye on your place," he said. "But I'd better get going."

"I'll see you later, I suppose," she said.

He nodded, his steely gaze meeting hers once more. "You can count on it."

As Emily walked back to her front door, she could feel his warm gaze enveloping her.

Safe. He made her feel so safe, so protected. It was a

shame they couldn't make this into something more...
lasting. When she unlocked the door and turned, Greg
lifted a hand in a wave, then got into his car.

Chapter Fourteen

On Monday, Greg sat in the hum of the station that filtered through his closed office door and glanced at the clock on the wall. It always amazed him how much time red tape could take up in a day. Picking up the file from "that 11-80," as it was being called around the station, he ran his finger down the page and stopped at a phone number. He hated making these sorts of calls—they were the kind that ended marriages.

After dialing the number, he tapped his pen on a yellow legal pad, listening to the ring on the other end.

"Hello, this is the Lindgren residence." It was a woman's voice, crisp and confident.

"Is this Mrs. Lindgren?" he asked.

"Yes, it is."

"Your husband is Senator Charles Lindgren?"

"Yes, he is. Who is this, please?" Wariness entered her tone.

"This is Chief Taylor from the Haggerston Police. I have a few questions for you. Is this a good time to talk?"

"The police?" He could hear the frown enter her voice. "What happened? Is something wrong?"

"I'm investigating a highway accident that occurred

a few weeks ago." He leaned back in his desk chair with a creak. He looked out his office window, his eyes moving up toward the blue summer sky.

"Oh, I see. Well, I have a few minutes. What can I do for you?"

"Does the name Jessica Shaw mean anything to you?" He flicked open a pen and began to doodle on the legal pad, drawing a series of stars and filling them in with black ink.

There was a pause. "No."

"Are you sure?"

Another pause. "Should it?"

"Not necessarily, but you don't sound certain. Have you heard the name before? Anywhere at all?"

"Did something happen to her?"

"Do you know her?"

"No, I don't know her, and no, I haven't heard her name before." She sighed. "But I'm also not a fool. Did something happen to this woman? How is this related to us?"

"She'd dead." Greg pushed himself back up with another creak and leaned his elbows on his desk. "She wasn't a friend of the family, then?"

"No, she isn't." The wariness was back. "She wasn't."

"This is going to be difficult, Mrs. Lindgren." Greg softened his tone. "I have to ask, though. Is there any possibility that your husband might have…had a friendship you weren't aware of?"

"My husband knows many people I don't. He's a politician." Her voice was tired. "That's part of the life. Chief Taylor, was it?"

"Yes, Chief Greg Taylor."

"Well, it's one of the things I've had to get used to, Chief."

"Affairs?"

Silence. He hadn't expected her to answer that one. She was a politician's wife, and if she was putting up with indiscretions in her marriage for the sake of appearances and position, she wasn't about to spill her secret sorrows to him. If politicians were smooth, then the spouses of politicians had to be smoother still.

"Mrs. Lindgren, I don't believe this young woman was murdered. It was a simple highway accident. There is no reason for us to believe otherwise, but I do have some questions I'd like to get answers to. I'd appreciate any help you could give me."

"Is this on the record?" she asked.

"Madam, there is no reason for it to be. Anything you say will never be repeated to the press. I can assure you."

She had a decision to make. She needed to weigh the damage of saying too much against the damage of appearing to be uncooperative with a police investigation. After a moment, he heard her sigh.

"My husband is a good man. He works hard. He cares about his constituents, and he is honest in his work."

"Yes, ma'am."

"He is also…" She paused. "Our relationship has had its trials, Chief. He works long hours and young, pretty girls tend to throw themselves at him. So yes, there have been some affairs. If you decide to dig, and you very well might, you will come up with infidelity. I've forgiven him, though, and I don't think he is being unfaithful now."

"How can you be sure?" he asked quietly.

She cleared her throat. "I can't be, can I? Not after a breach in trust like that, but things are different now. Back then, we were awfully distanced. He worked, and I shopped. Now we talk, and we're much closer. I don't think it's possible right now. I'd know it. I'd feel the distance again."

Greg nodded. "Okay. Thank you for your time, Mrs. Lindgren. It is much appreciated."

"Please, Chief. Be discreet."

"You have my word."

As he hung up the phone, he tapped his pen on the legal pad again, pursing his lips. It didn't seem likely that Jessica had been a surrogate mother for the couple. If she had been, there would have been a much bigger emotional response from Mrs. Lindgren, considering Cora would be her daughter by all rights, if that were the case. He had to mentally cross that option off his list. Either Mrs. Lindgren didn't know Jessica Shaw, or she was a phenomenal actress. It was remotely possible, but not likely.

On the pad he wrote in block letters: MISTRESS.

He wasn't as optimistic as Mrs. Lindgren. Or Emily, for that matter. Part of him felt as if he should apologize to Emily. She wasn't going to want to see her cousin in that light, but more than that, the senator may well be Cora's biological father, giving a rich and powerful man more right to the baby than anyone else so far

I can't be the guy who crushes her with this...

But the reality was that he had a job to do, regardless of his personal feelings toward Emily Shaw.

Emily looked out her front window as the police cruiser drove slowly by. It was a relief to know that the Haggerston police were looking out for her and Cora, and she was grateful to Greg. If he were a different guy, he would never have taken her seriously—but Greg was different in a good way. He was intuitive and gentle underneath that tough cop shell he held together so well. Haggerston was lucky to have him. She was lucky—

She stopped herself. No, she didn't have him. She was lucky to have a friend like him. That was a more honest statement.

"I've been considering an epidural," Beth said from where she sat on the couch, her swollen feet propped up. She flipped the page in a parenting magazine.

"Oh?" Emily turned around and shot her friend a grin. "What made you change your mind?"

"Terror." Beth turned another page.

"What does Howard think?"

Beth looked up from the magazine and cast her an icy look. "Howard will be grateful when I bring this child into the world and shut his mouth about the rest."

Emily laughed and held her hands up in defeat. "Getting nervous, huh?"

Beth nodded. "I've been watching natural-childbirth videos online."

"Oh, bad idea!" Emily grimaced. "Even I know that."

"Yeah, well, I think I want to be numb from the waist down, thank you very much."

"No judgment here." Emily looked toward Cora, nestled in her bassinet and sleeping deeply. She envied Beth, even with the labor and pain she had to look forward to.

"Now, about that baby shower." Beth looked up with a twinkle in her eye. "How do you think Greg will fare?"

"He's pretty resilient." Emily chuckled, but a mental image arose of Greg very uncomfortable and irritated at being in the middle of baby talk and silly games. She suddenly wasn't so sure.

"Oh, he'll be fine." Beth seemed to read her mind, or perhaps the deflated look on her face. "It's a couple of hours in the afternoon. Besides, he wants to keep an eye on you, doesn't he?"

"True, he does, but I'm probably safest in the middle of friends at a shower, don't you think?"

"Definitely, but he agreed to this long before that creep ever showed up." Beth grinned over at her. "There's more to it than protecting you, and you know it."

Emily laughed. "You want this to be more serious than it is, Beth."

"I know, I know." Beth turned her attention back to the magazine. "I think you're both stubborn."

"You can't force things, Beth." Emily sighed.

"If you could see things the way everyone watching you sees them…" Beth looked up with an amused smile tickling her lips. "But never mind. You're a big girl and don't need me meddling."

"Thanks." Emily rolled her eyes and laughed. Beth was well-intentioned. She wanted to see Emily married to a great guy and settling into a domestic life like she had. But not everyone was so lucky to find the perfect man for her in high school, get married and have his baby.

"We need cookies," Emily announced and, pushing herself back to her feet, she escaped to the kitchen to find them.

Chapter Fifteen

Greg couldn't help but smile when he saw Emily standing in her doorway in a red polka-dot dress, her dark hair pulled back into a glossy ponytail and a friendly twinkle in her eyes.

"Hi, Greg." She stepped back to let him in with a bright smile. "Thanks for being such a good sport."

He looked at her uneasily. "What am I expecting, exactly? Can't say I've ever been to a baby shower before."

"Oh, some silly games, some snack food, some cake. It won't be too terrifying." She cast him a teasing glance as she bent over Cora to pick her up.

"Somehow I don't feel so reassured." He laughed. "So where are we headed?"

"The Cedar Glen Elementary School. They're holding it in the gym there."

Greg nodded, then he inwardly grimaced as he thought of something. "I was supposed to bring you a present, wasn't I?"

Emily turned around, the baby in her arms, her bright eyes meeting his with an easy smile. "Greg, you coming with me to this thing *is* my present. Trust me. Thanks for just coming along."

He smiled back and gave her a shrug. "My pleasure." He resisted the urge to pull a strand of hair away from her forehead. "Ready?"

She picked up a diaper bag and grabbed her keys from a bowl by the door. "Ready."

Putting the car seat into the back of the vehicle was much easier this time around, and before much time had passed, they were pulling out of her drive and heading back toward town. The scent of Emily's light perfume filled the car, and he leaned his head back as he drove, enjoying her company. She had no idea the kind of effect she had on him, he knew. How could she? He'd never told her that she calmed his nerves by just being there, that her smile made him want to grin like a teenager and that he thought about her during the day far more often than was prudent for a man trying to keep things uncomplicated. But there it was.

As they settled into the car, Greg's cell phone rang. He glanced at the number. It was Shady Pines.

"I'd better take this." He shot her an apologetic smile, then picked up the call. "Hello, Chief Taylor here."

"Hi, Chief." Fran's voice was low. "I thought I should give you a call."

"What's going on?" he asked.

"When I got into my shift this afternoon, I found your mom sedated."

"Sedated?" He lowered his voice. "Why?"

"The nurse I replaced told me that she got confused and was very upset. She didn't understand why she was here in Shady Pines, and she wanted to go home. She was fighting everyone, and they sedated her so she could rest and forget."

"No one called me."

"It isn't specified on your mother's chart that they

should, so if there is a nurse on shift who doesn't know you, they wouldn't know what we normally do."

"Has this happened before?" he asked.

"No, she's never gotten this agitated before. She was always relatively calm."

Unless I was visiting, upsetting her, he thought wryly.

"I want to be called the next time this happens," he said. "Make sure that goes on her chart."

"That's what I needed from you, Chief." Fran's tone turned professional and efficient. "I'll mark it down."

"Thanks." Greg took a deep breath. "So she's sleeping now?"

"Yes, she's sleeping peacefully. More than likely, she'll wake up in a happy frame of mind. She'll be all right."

"Thanks, Fran. Keep in touch."

As he dropped his cell phone back into his pocket, he exhaled a pent-up breath and started the car.

"Everything okay?" Emily asked softly.

Greg glanced over at her to see her dark eyes trained on him. He nodded and put the car into gear to pull out of the drive. The wheels crunched over the gravel as they headed out toward the main road. Emily settled into the seat but still watched him.

"It's okay," he said.

"A problem with your mom?"

He shot her a half smile. "They sedated her when she got upset. I don't like that."

Emily nodded. "She must have been pretty scared."

"That's what I thought, and pinning her down and coming at her with a needle—" He stopped.

"Do you think they did that?"

He shook his head. "Well, if she was upset, they certainly didn't pass her a pill in a spoonful of applesauce."

Emily nodded. "No, you're probably right. So they'll call you next time, instead of sedating her?"

"That's what Fran said."

"What will you do when they call?"

Her question was posed in such a soft voice that Greg almost didn't hear it. He had no idea what he'd do. He'd go down there and pray that somehow he could distract her or show her that she was safe. He'd do his best, even though his best didn't seem to amount to a whole lot lately when it came to his mother. He signaled and pulled onto the main road back toward Haggerston.

"I have no idea." Glancing over at her, he pressed his lips together in thought. "Unless you'd be willing to come with me."

"Do you think I could help?"

The fields stretched peacefully out on either side of the highway, one side golden with canola and the other spotted with a herd of cattle. Truth be told, he had no idea what would help. He was hoping, more than anything.

"She trusts you."

Emily was silent for a moment, and when he glanced in her direction, he discovered her eyes on him, her brows furrowed in concern. "If you want me there, just call."

"Sometimes it's just a matter of calming her down. The nurses always managed to before. But—" he swallowed, memories of her terrified fits running through his mind "—but she's not the sweet woman you met before…not all the time. She gets scared. She yells and hits."

Emily didn't look alarmed in the least. "I would, too, if I thought someone was going to pin me down and ram a needle into my arm."

Greg caught her eye as she shot him a sympathetic smile.

"I don't want to ask too much. It isn't easy dealing with dementia."

She gave a faint shrug. "I teach twenty five-year-olds at once. I'm pretty tough."

His mother's words suddenly echoed through his mind. *You've got one tough mama, sweetheart. We'll be all right.* He glanced at her, taking in the dark hair and creamy complexion. When it came to strong women, he'd been fortunate in his lifetime. His mother had been as strong as they came, and Emily, it seemed, was made up of the same kind of undaunted determination. He swallowed the emotion rising in his throat.

Cora began to fuss in the backseat, and Emily turned around to pop the soother back into her little searching mouth. For just a moment, as Emily leaned around the seat, her glossy, dark hair rested on his shoulder, and he inhaled the fruity scent of her shampoo. Her warm, soft arm pressed against his for a moment as she reached, and her gentle voice, directed at Cora, sounded soft and low in his ear. His heart sped up, and he took a deep breath.

Uncomplicated, he reminded himself. *Aiming at uncomplicated here.*

For the life of him, though, he couldn't remember *why.*

The gym at Cedar Glen Elementary wasn't very large, the far side of it boasting a stage with thick, orange curtains closed. The floor had all the basketball and volleyball lines drawn onto the old hardwood, and the door echoed ominously as she pushed it open, Cora's car seat in one hand, her arm already aching from the weight of it.

"Hey, there she is!" Beth called. The far corner by the stage was decorated with balloons and streamers, a snack table filled with goodies set up and a cake already on display, and under the table she could see the gifts peeking through. Emily smiled self-consciously.

"Hello," she called back.

She could feel the warmth of Greg's chest behind her, and it was comforting to know that she wasn't stepping into this gym on her own, the one lonely wheel in the midst of all these couples. The other teachers and their significant others had arrived, and they turned to smile and wave, little paper plates of veggies and dip and plastic cups of punch keeping their hands full.

As they approached, her teacher friends came up to shake Greg's hand and look into Cora's car seat.

"Isn't she precious? Just look at her!"

"And who is this?" someone burst out.

"This is Cora."

"No, I mean *this*."

Emily blinked and looked up to see that the woman was referring to Greg, not the baby. She laughed and felt her face heat in a blush.

"Oh, this is Greg, or Chief Taylor—"

"Hi, I'm Greg." Greg put his hand out for a shake. "Nice to meet you."

The hellos and baby admiration went on for some time, her friends and colleagues coming to give their congratulations on Cora. Most of them didn't realize the complicated situation this was, and the few who did were diplomatic about it, for which Emily was grateful. Greg's presence was more help than he probably realized. Just having him there to smoothly smile, shake hands and make small talk took some of the pressure off her.

"Hi," Beth said, tugging Emily aside. "So you two

came!" She looked over at Greg, beaming in delight with the whole arrangement.

"Yes, yes." Emily laughed. "It's easier having him here. Look how he managed to get past Mildred Kuchka."

Beth nodded in admiration of the feat. Mildred was talkative and generally abrasive. They could only imagine that when she'd been hired some thirty-odd years ago, she'd been nicer, but that many years with grade-four students seemed to have chipped instead of polished her, leaving her bitter and far too direct with everyone she met. Greg, however, had managed to intercept her, make some small talk and effectively send her on her way without Mildred even knowing how it had happened. She looked slightly stunned and charmed by the whole event, making Emily cover her mouth to hide a laugh.

"Well, let's get started." Beth glanced at her watch. "We have to be out of here by seven-thirty. There's a volleyball game scheduled." Beth raised her voice to her playground level and clapped her hands sharply. "Okay, everyone. Let's take our seats!"

A chuckle rippled through the place but they complied, and Beth laughed and shot Emily a bashful look. "I haven't gotten grade two out of my system."

Everyone moved to the circle of chairs and got settled, Emily's chair marked by a halo of balloons rising from it. Greg settled down next to her, and Cora dozed peacefully in the car seat at her feet. Sitting there in the circle of well-wishers, she couldn't help but feel amazed at all of this. In a few short weeks she'd gone from being the single kindergarten teacher of room 12 to being a new mother at a baby shower. Her life had done a 180-degree turn, and here she was, wondering if it would last or evaporate. She glanced over at Greg, and he caught her eye with a half smile.

Some introductions and kind words about Emily's teaching abilities and her way with children left Emily feeling uncomfortable in the middle of the smiling attention. They meant well, but she hated this, and she was relieved when Beth heaved herself to her feet and rested her hands on top of her belly.

"We have one game to play before we open presents," Beth announced. "And this is a game for couples, but not for the faint of heart."

Emily looked over at Greg, and he gave her a wink. If she wasn't mistaken, he looked as though he was enjoying himself, but he was alert in a way that she recognized. He was watching, his eyes moving over the guests in a casual but observant fashion. He also looked quickly from door to door around the gym. Seeming satisfied for the moment, he turned back to Emily.

"No passing the baby around tonight, okay?" he said softly.

"Not safe?" she murmured back.

"Not entirely."

She nodded. Nina emerged from the kitchen, adjacent to the gym, with a platter of open baby-food jars held aloft. She moved like a skilled waitress, something that amused Emily to no end.

"There are four flavors of baby food," Beth explained. "Nina is going to give you four jars, and it's up to the men to guess the flavor. Ladies, you're doing the spooning, and men, you're doing the guessing."

There was a titter of appreciation from the women and a humored groan from the men. One of the male teachers called out, "I thought the women were supposed to be the experts on these things" and received a good-natured swat from his wife.

"See?" Emily glanced at Greg with a grin. "I told you this would be work."

"How bad can it be?" Greg moved his chair to face Emily and Cora. He gave her a playful grin. "Babies eat it."

The jars were passed around with paper taped over the labels, and Emily sat with the four little jars in front of her and a baby spoon in her hand. Greg looked down at the jars, some misgiving betrayed in his eyes.

"All right, ladies, give the men a spoonful from jar number one," Beth called out joyfully.

Emily glanced down at jar number one. It looked yellowish and a bit lumpy. She sniffed it and gave Greg a look of sympathy. "This one is cruelty." She spooned a little bit of it into his mouth and watched him make a face.

"Oh, that's awful. It has corn in it. Okay, give me another spoon."

"You sure?" She looked down into the jar dubiously.

"I can take it. Come on."

She gave him another bite, and he swished it around his mouth thoughtfully. Emily cringed and watched him with some trepidation.

"Chicken and corn. Possibly some rice."

Emily wrote down his answer on a little piece of paper and turned her attention to the next jar. It was brownish-red, and when she spooned a little bit into Greg's mouth, he nodded thoughtfully.

"Another bite."

"Not sure what it is?"

"Oh, I know what it is. It's apple strawberry. This one is good."

She laughed and gave him an extra-big spoonful to wash down the chicken and rice. Emily looked around the room at the other couples. The men were making faces, and the women were laughing in good fun. What was it about babies and all the little necessities that came with them that bonded couples together so perfectly? She looked back at Greg to see him watching her with gentleness in his eyes.

"You're a good sport," she said softly.

"It's worth it."

She blushed at that, her eyes flickering up to meet his. He held her gaze and gave a faint shrug, then nodded toward the next jar.

"I'm ready."

Emily scooped a healthy spoonful of the next option into his mouth. The minute it went in, he spat it out into a napkin.

"That bad?" She laughed and looked down at Cora to see her eyes fixed on Greg.

"Cora, take notes." Greg made a face. "Never eat pureed lima beans. Just don't go there."

"You have to make it look good, Greg," Emily teased. "That way she'll know that healthy food is delicious."

Greg rolled his eyes and laughed. "That's where I draw the line. I'll eat the baby food, but you can't make me like it."

"We have a winner over here!" Nina called, holding up the hand of one of the husbands.

"Oh, thank goodness." Greg laughed out loud. "I don't even care what the last jar is."

There was laughter as the older man was presented with his prize—a trucker's hat that read My Baby Loves Me. The evening went on with present opening, followed by cake cutting. Emily cuddled Cora close when she woke up, and she received all sorts of attention from the women. At the end of the party, as Greg helped Emily to gather up the generous gifts from her colleagues, Mildred made her way over and bent down to the car seat where Cora was sleeping once more, her little tummy full of milk.

"Well, isn't she a sweet thing," Mildred said. "A shame her mother is dead."

"Yes, Jessica was my cousin," Emily explained.

"So the baby is yours now?"

"I'm her guardian. There are a few hoops to jump through still."

"So she isn't yours?" Mildred looked up and drilled Emily with an icy look, daring her to lie to her.

"I'm her guardian," Emily repeated. She could feel the anger and hurt rising up inside of her, but she did her best to push it back. A scene with Mildred Kuchka wasn't going to do anyone any good.

"So she might go to someone else for good, then?" Mildred pressed.

"I hope not." She could feel her eyes misting with tears. Yes, the truth was that Cora might go to someone else. After Emily had fallen in love with her, bonded with her and nurtured her, she might have to say goodbye yet. It was the cold, hard truth that she'd been avoiding all this time, doing her best to push aside until absolutely necessary.

"Well, if she goes to someone else, you can send my gift along with her. No need to return it." Mildred straightened herself to her full six feet and folded her bony hands in front of her as if that settled the matter.

Emily took a deep, albeit shaky, breath, but before she could speak, Greg came up beside her and fixed Mildred with a look of his own.

"Mrs. Kuchka," he said, his voice low and official. "Do you have any personal knowledge about custody cases?"

"Me?" She made a sound somewhere between a harrumph and cough. "No. No, I don't."

"Ah." He nodded curtly. "Well, then, that will be all."

The older woman blinked twice, nodded and stepped away. Emily cast him a grateful look.

"Sometimes it helps to treat it like a crime scene," he said.

"I'll remember that. Not sure I could pull it off, though."

Emily followed him, laden down with gifts, out toward the car. She was silent, still uncertain of her emotions. When they settled in the car, windows down, Emily closed her eyes, trying to push the sadness away. She felt Greg's strong, warm hand on hers.

"Are you okay?"

She opened her eyes. "I'm all right."

"You're a terrible liar." His gaze was sympathetic. "She got to you, didn't she?"

Emily nodded. "Doesn't take much lately." She felt the tears rising again, this time in response to his kindness, and as they spilled over onto her cheeks, Greg reached out and slid his arm around her, pulling her onto his broad, strong chest.

She was surprised by the movement, both by his strength and by the tender gesture. He stroked her hair away from her face while she cried and leaned a cheek on top of her head. She could smell the soft musk of his aftershave, and to simply be held while she cried out her grief was something she hadn't even realized she'd been missing until she felt how warm and safe it was in his arms. As she sniffled and wiped her tears, pushing up away from that strong, comforting chest, he released her and tucked a stray strand of hair out of her face.

"Better?" he asked softly.

"Much." She blushed, embarrassed to have cried on him, let alone in front of him. "It's been hard lately."

"I know." His eyes met hers, and they exchanged a look of sorrow. He had his own heartbreak lately with his sick mother, she realized. He understood her better than she knew.

"I can do this," Emily said quietly. "I can. I'm a grown woman, and I'm strong. I can raise her alone, and I know she'll be loved and she'll thrive. But that doesn't mean it doesn't get really hard sometimes."

He nodded. "I feel it, too. I'm a grown man, but when it comes to my mom being sick, it's like it taps into the little boy inside of me. I hate it, and I can't change it."

"Someone with you makes all the difference, doesn't it?"

He smiled, the lines around his eyes crinkling. "Sure does."

"We'll be okay, Greg," she said with a nod. "We're grown-ups, after all. We can do this."

He looked ready to say something, but then he closed his mouth and nodded. Putting the key into the ignition, he started the car.

"Let's get you girls home," he said, and as he pulled out of the parking space, she realized wistfully that his strong arms were the most comforting place she'd been in a very long time.

Chapter Sixteen

The next morning, while Emily was sorting through the gifts she was given at the shower, her mind kept going back to Mildred Kuchka's comment. What, exactly, was she expected to do with these generous gifts if Cora wasn't left in her care? She sighed, picking up a frilly little dress with a matching lace bonnet. Everyone had been so kind. She'd been given clothing, toys, a cake made of diapers and even a stroller. Everything she needed—but she felt awkward looking at all of it, afraid to open the boxes or break the packaging, lest a week from now she was no longer the new mom. What happened then? Was she supposed to give them all their gifts back, complete with a note of apology for wasting their time and good intentions?

She put down the little dress and picked up another outfit—tiny jeans and a T-shirt that read I Love My Mommy. She put it down in the pile and rubbed her hands over her face. The little outfit would fit Cora now, but would it fit a week from now, after the court hearing? That was the irony.

The phone rang, and Emily stretched to reach the

handset. The number on the display belonged to the school.

"Hello?"

"Hello, Miss Shaw, this is Principal Edwards."

Her boss. Emily leaned back on her heels. "Hi, what can I do for you?"

"I was wondering if we could talk about your plans this coming school year," he said slowly. "I understand you have a baby now. Congratulations, by the way."

"Thanks." Emily smiled wanly. "Actually, I don't know yet. I'm the guardian for the baby, but there is a court hearing coming up. I'm being contested for guardianship."

"Ah." There was an awkward silence. "When is the hearing?"

"In about a week."

"Ah." Another silence. "The thing is, Miss Shaw, I'm leaving for the summer in two days. I need to have this sorted out before I go. If you're going to want parental leave, we need to get the proper forms sorted out today."

"Today?" Emily looked around herself. "What did you have in mind?"

"Could you come by the school for a couple of hours this morning?" he asked.

Emily's mind immediately moved to Cora. She'd need some childcare for this meeting. Principal Edwards was a very stoic man, and a fussing baby or a dirty diaper, a bottle—those were things she knew weren't going to be useful in a meeting about her career.

"Sure. I'll sort something out and be there in about an hour."

Hanging up the phone, she mentally went through her checklist of people she trusted with Cora. Her parents were away for the week on a cruise, Nina was at work, Beth was crib shopping today. With her cousins' appearance at her parents' house the last time she went out without Cora, she was nervous about a repeat performance with other family members.

That left Greg, the one person she knew could and would deal with her pushy cousin if it ever came to that…but would he babysit?

Greg stood by the coffeepot, watching the fresh coffee drip. It was one of those unpredictable mornings. It had started with a lost elderly man wandering around in his boxer shorts. His family called the station shortly after he was found, but Greg had ended up cornered with the old fellow, trying to answer his quavering questions. "Where am I? Who took my pants?"

There was a domestic disturbance where a husband was getting violent with his wife. She called the station, and Benny went out directly to arrest the man. After bringing him in, the wife begged to have him released, and then decided to lodge an official complaint against Benny for having done his job. Official complaints were a ridiculous amount of paperwork and, of course, couldn't be ignored, so after wading his way through half of it, he was here at the coffeepot, waiting for a fresh cup.

He heard the tap of heels coming up behind him, and he turned to see Emily, Cora in her arms, coming toward him.

"Hi." He couldn't help the smile that came to his face. She looked great in a pair of tan slacks, a white blouse and a mauve silk scarf flung around her neck. Cora was chewing on the end of it.

"Greg, I've got a favor to ask." She looked downright penitent. "I don't have anyone else I can trust right now, not with the hearing and everything. I need to go into work for a few minutes. It'll be an hour or two, tops, but I can't bring Cora." She stopped and looked at him hopefully.

"Oh…" He wasn't quite sure what to say.

"Would you watch her for me? I promise, I won't do this to you again. After the hearing I have several aunts who would love to get their hands on her for a morning."

"You want me to babysit?" He looked around uncertainly.

"Would you?" She fell into silence, her dark eyes meeting his while she waited for his response. His first instinct was to say a decided no, but her pleading eyes and Cora blinking at him, the end of the scarf still in her mouth, left him drained of fight.

"I'm going to be working on paperwork for most of the morning," he admitted. "I suppose I could keep an eye on Sweet pea."

"Oh, thanks, Greg." She exhaled a sigh of relief. "Thank you, thank you."

She leaned over and kissed his cheek, then passed Cora into his arms. She also deposited the diaper bag and another contraption on the floor beside him. "There are diapers and bottles and a couple changes of clothes, if you need them. She's already had her morning bottle and shouldn't want to eat again for a while, but if she seems hungry, it's there. She's been a bit fussy this morning with some diaper rash, so make sure that you use the diaper cream when you change her." She bent down and kissed Cora's cheek. "Speaking of which, she's wet."

With a brilliant smile, Emily turned and her heels clicked a little staccato beat back out of the station, that silk scarf fluttering out behind her, sodden at one end with baby drool. She turned before she pushed open the door and smiled lovingly at Cora, then slipped out into the morning sunlight. Greg stood there in silence, watching her go. He looked mutely down at Cora.

"Hey, is that Sweet pea?" Benny came into the room and beelined over to where Greg stood. "How are you?" He bent down to her level and made a fish face for her benefit. Cora blinked and let out a soft coo.

"It looks like I'm—" Greg stopped himself. Somehow, using the word *babysitting* felt so wrong. Instead, he said weakly, "She's wet."

"Better get to it, then, Chief," Benny said, shooting up into a standing position again and heading off in the direction of his desk.

Greg smiled wryly. That seemed about right. When the baby was cute and dry, everyone wanted her. When she was in need of some diaper changing, her fans evaporated.

"Tough life, kiddo," he said softly, lifting Cora higher onto his shoulder. "Let's get you changed."

Back in his office, Greg dropped the diaper bag and the odd cloth contraption Emily had left with it on a chair and cleared off the middle of his wide desk. It would have to do. After a few minutes of one-handed wrangling, he managed to get a blanket down on the desktop, then laid Cora down on top. He looked down at her uncertainly. He reached over and pressed a button.

"Yes, Chief?"

"Joyce, would you come in here, please?"

There was a short silence. "To change the diaper, Chief?"

She'd caught him. "Yes?" He didn't mean to sound so uncertain. He heard laughter outside the door, and he grimaced.

"I'm sorry, sir, that isn't in my job description."

Fine, fine, he thought to himself and settled about removing the wet diaper. She wore a little dress, so that was uncomplicated enough, but when he tried to lift the tabs of the diaper, he found them stickier than he'd thought. He pulled harder. Nothing.

"Huh," he muttered to himself. "Is there a trick to this?"

He looked at the tabs from a different angle. It should be simple. He tugged a couple more times and looked down into Cora's serious little face.

"You're stuck in there," he told her.

She kicked her legs hopefully. A wet diaper couldn't be comfortable. A diaper was nothing more than some plastic and cotton padding, so it shouldn't be too hard to tear. He grabbed the diaper on two sides, and with a grunt of effort, he began to pull. The diaper stretched, but it was oddly strong.

What are these things made of? Titanium?

He got a better grip and pulled again, using a movement like stretching a spring. His biceps bulged with the effort, and Cora cooed out her delight at the loosening diaper. The material began to stretch and tear, much to his satisfaction. He heard his office door opening and he froze, the diaper nearly torn in two between his fists.

Joyce stood there in the doorway, a look of shocked amazement on her face. "Chief?"

He looked at her. "Yes, Joyce?"

"What are you doing?"

"Changing a diaper."

"They come off without you having to turn into the Incredible Hulk, you know."

Greg rolled his eyes. "Normally, but not this time."

Tearing the rest of the diaper free, he held it aloft. It was in two pieces, held together by some stretched cotton. Cora looked up at it mutely. Joyce also looked at the diaper in silence, regarding it with solemn respect.

"There," Greg said, balling it up as best he could and lobbing it over to his garbage can. "And now, the easy part."

It didn't turn out to be quite as easy as he'd thought, but Joyce gave him a hand, and before too long, Cora was diapered and happy again.

Joyce held up the cloth contraption next to the diaper bag. "This'll help."

"What is it?"

"A baby carrier. You just pop her inside and wear it like a backward backpack." She brought it over and held it out.

"Huh." He looked it over and regarded Cora. "Do you want this?" he asked her dubiously.

"Trust me." Joyce slid it onto his chest and disappeared behind him, tightening and adjusting some straps. Then she came around and slid Cora into the gaping front pocket. She settled into the little seat just below his chin, and he looked down onto Cora's downy red curls. It seemed like a pretty efficient arrangement.

"Chief?" Nancy poked her head into the office. "I've got the court order to release the rest of Jessica Shaw's banking information. We can follow that money now."

"Excellent." Greg patted Cora's back through the carrier. "Let's get started on that."

The rest of the morning ebbed away with more paperwork, and an hour later found Greg seated at his desk, leaning back so that Cora could sleep more comfortably. She snored softly, one little hand clutching a fistful of shirt. He'd been less than enthusiastic about this initially, but now he found himself enjoying it. He'd sat in this position at his desk before, one hand on his computer mouse as he ran through some emails, but having a baby snuggled against his chest made the whole thing a lot more relaxing.

His phone rang, and he picked it up on the first ring.

"Hello, Chief Taylor here." He kept his voice low, not wanting to disturb Cora's sleep.

"Hi, Chief. This is Lana Heibert from First Colonial Bank. We received the court order for the information about those deposits."

"Great." Greg was suddenly alert, and he picked up a pen. "What can you tell me?"

"They all came from the same account, belonging to a Mr. Charles Lindgren."

"Are you sure about that?" Greg asked. "Is it possible to make it appear that way?"

"No, this is very direct—no attempts to hide anything." He could hear some clicking in the background on her end of the phone. "This is a personal account. He has joint accounts with his wife, but this is a private savings account."

"Thank you," Greg said, a satisfied smile coming to his face.

"My pleasure. Give me a call if you need anything else."

"Will do."

As he hung up the phone, Greg stifled the urge to laugh out loud. It was almost too easy, but he was glad to be getting ahead. It looked as if the senator was in this up to his neck. Pushing himself to his feet and supporting Cora's head with one hand, he headed out of his office toward Nancy's desk. Two of the officers were laughing loudly together by the coffee, and Cora gurgled and wriggled. Greg pointed at the two officers ominously.

"Sleeping baby, guys," he barked. "Quiet down."

"Sorry, Chief."

Voices lowered in obedience, and he gave a satisfied nod as Cora resettled into her nap. Making his way over to Nancy's desk, he found Benny there, too, sinking his teeth into a doughnut.

"All right, we've got a break." Greg leaned onto the edge of Nancy's desk. "It looks like the large deposits in Jessica Shaw's checking account did come from one of the senator's accounts."

"Aha." Benny grinned. "I knew it."

"So what do we do now?" Nancy asked. "Bring him in for questioning?"

"For what?" Greg shook his head. "We have no reason to suspect that Jessica was murdered. That was a highway accident, not foul play. But I do want some answers here."

Benny popped the last of his doughnut into his mouth and talked around it. "What about the guy following her?"

"It'll all come together when I'm done with this. I'm not sure how innocent the senator will be, but we'll have answers, at least."

Greg looked up as he heard someone coming into the station. It was Emily.

"One more thing," Greg said, keeping his voice low. "Until I say otherwise, this information is strictly confidential. I don't want Emily—Miss Shaw—knowing about it just yet."

"Sure thing, Chief." They both nodded, then looked up as Emily approached.

Greg couldn't help but smile as Emily cocked her head to one side in order to look at Cora's little face. Her eyes turned tender, and she brushed one finger over the infant's cheek, then raised her dark eyes to meet his.

"Thanks, Greg. I appreciate this." Her voice was low and soft, and he found himself momentarily speechless.

"Oh, we love Sweet pea around here," Benny said with a slow grin. "And the chief here has quite a way with diapers."

Greg cast Benny a scathing look, which only made the big man's smile broader.

"What's that smell, Chief?" Nancy asked, frowning.

Greg could smell the faint odor, too. He wasn't sure. It smelled eerily like a wet diaper, but the source wasn't Cora. His garbage can in the office? Wow. That was pungent.

"I'll tell you what," Greg said, turning to Benny with a wide smile of his own. "I'm going to let you find the source of that smell, Benny. I'm off for lunch."

Benny's grin dropped, and Greg couldn't help but chuckle. Revenge was best served wet…and in a diaper. Emily glanced up at him.

"Could I offer you a sandwich at my place? A thanks for babysitting."

"Absolutely."

Heading for the door, Cora in the baby carrier against his chest and Emily next to him, her soft perfume tugging him along, he couldn't help but feel a little spring in his step—a spring he'd better not be getting used to.

Chapter Seventeen

Back at her home, Emily stood at the kitchen counter making two bacon, lettuce and tomato sandwiches on toast. She was good at BLTs, and she enjoyed arranging them just so. They were the sort of lunch she made for herself when she was tired and in need of some comfort food without much effort. She could hear the sound of a dog barking outside, and as she worked, crisscrossing bacon strips, she glanced over at Cora, snuggled happily in her bassinet.

"So do you know what you're going to do?" Greg asked. "Job-wise, I mean."

"I have no idea," she admitted with a shrug. "Basically, I've applied for parental leave just in case I have Cora with me, but—" She let the rest of the sentence hang.

He nodded thoughtfully, but didn't say anything. His eyes were trained out the window, watching some robins playing in the grass, and she wondered what he was preoccupied with.

"So how was babysitting?" she asked.

He looked back at her, a twinkle in his eye. "I liked

it." He leaned his elbow on the counter and snagged a strip of bacon off the plate, taking a crispy bite.

"Honestly?" She shot him an amused look at his thievery.

"Honestly. I mean, I'm pretty sure they're all gossiping about me like crazy right now, but it was good." He chuckled. "I had a bit of an adventure changing her diaper."

"What happened?"

"I don't look good in this story." He shook his head and laughed softly. "Let's just leave it."

Emily shook her head and smothered a laugh, putting the tops on the sandwiches with a satisfying pat. She slid his plate in front of him at the counter, watching his eyes hungrily light up. They stood together at the counter, their food in front of them and the afternoon sunlight pooling on the floor behind them. Outside the window, the robins were poking around for worms. It was quiet and peaceful.

"Thanks for this," Greg said, taking a big bite of the sandwich.

Emily smiled and took a bite of her own, the saltiness of the crisp bacon mingling with tangy mayonnaise. She was hungrier than she'd thought, and after a couple of minutes, she'd devoured half her sandwich. Wiping her lips on a napkin, she glanced over at Greg.

"This is nice," she said.

"Food?" he asked wryly.

"Company."

"Hmm," he agreed, sinking his teeth into another bite. He chewed and swallowed. "Your company, especially."

"You know, Greg, I don't think I'll be able to just go back to the way things were."

He looked at her, worry creasing his forehead. "What do you mean?"

"With Cora."

"Oh." He nodded quickly. "Of course."

"What did you think I meant?"

He blushed slightly and shook it off. "It doesn't matter. What were you saying about Cora?"

Emily looked over at Cora. She grunted softly in her sleep, and her diaper rustled as she stretched out her little legs. Even sleeping, Cora was a heart stealer. Emily pulled her eyes away and put her attention back into her sandwich.

"Well, I don't think I can just go back to being the single, cheerful kindergarten teacher if this doesn't happen. I want a family. I want a husband and kids and crayon on my walls." She looked wistfully toward the bassinet again. "I adore her, and if she won't be mine, I'm going to grieve, but it's more than that. I know what I want now, and I'm not going to be happy without it."

Greg's expression clouded, and he sat in silence for a long moment. There was something about the way he sat, so self-controlled, that she could feel something unspoken change between them.

"What's wrong?" she asked quietly.

He lifted his eyes to meet hers sadly. "It's okay. You're telling the truth."

"About wanting kids?" she asked hesitantly.

"I guess I was hoping you might consider me your consolation prize if it didn't work out according to plan." His eyes lingered on hers for a moment.

"Are you saying you were hoping I wouldn't be able to keep Cora?" she asked cautiously.

"No!" He shook his head, his eyes sparking with emotion. "You two belong together. I know that. Everyone knows that. I just… Look, I know I have no future with you. You're Cora's mother now, and you want kids. I know that. I accept it. It just— I don't know what to say.…"

Emily was silent, stunned. She swallowed hard and looked at him, his blue eyes filled with pain and the muscles in his forearms flexing as he breathed slow, controlled breaths. He pulled a strip of bacon out of the last half of his sandwich.

"But why—" She stopped herself short, then sighed. "But why not give it a try?"

As the question rolled off her tongue, she had a mental image of doing this all the time—eating sandwiches by the counter, tag-teaming in taking care of Cora, being each other's dates to important events… just being together. What was so wrong with that? What was so wrong with falling in love and getting married like everyone else did? What was so wrong with having a family?

He looked over at her, and by the look on his face, he was imagining something similar. He dropped the bacon onto his plate.

"I think about that a lot lately," he admitted slowly. "Trust me, I'd love to plan vacations with you, come home to you, raise Cora with you and be able to pull you into my arms and…" His voice trailed away.

And? She longed to hear the end of that thought, but she didn't dare ask. She imagined his soft lips coming down on hers, his arms winding around her in a strong hug and being able to melt into his embrace. She swallowed and shook away the image in her mind.

Instead, she said weakly, "Me, too."

He looked up, a smile creeping over his face. "We both seem to want the same thing, sort of."

"Then why don't we do it?" she asked. "Why not take a chance?"

"It's complicated." He sighed. He wiped his fingers on a napkin and stood up, his badge on his chest glistening in the afternoon light.

"Your job."

"It's more than a job." His voice grew stronger and he took a deep breath. "It's who I am. It's who my dad was. It's in my blood. I can't just walk away from it, and I can't put another family through what mine went through—what I went through. I might have been able to fight my way out, but there are kids who kill themselves from bullying. It's not just about missing a father figure. It's about more than that. It's about surviving without a father figure. What am I supposed to do take on a family that I can't guarantee I'll be around to protect?"

"But who says the same thing will happen?" Emily shook her head. "There is no prophecy of doom over your head saying you're going to die young."

Greg didn't answer, but she could feel him steeling, hardening. He looked over at her, his eyes almost pleading with her to understand. "We do want different things, Emily. I can't be a dad. I can get married, sure! I can be a husband, but kids are fragile. I can't put another child through that. I'd never forgive myself for being so selfish."

Emily turned away. Selfish. Is that what being a loving husband and father was—selfish? Why couldn't he just open his eyes and see what they had in front of them? How often in life did this kind of chance at love present itself? Did this sort of thing happen more than once in a lifetime?

"Okay, so now you're mad at me," he said.

"I'm not mad." Truth be told, she wasn't thrilled, either. She turned around and gave him a level look.

"You look mad." He gave her a tentative smile.

"I don't get it, Greg. It's not my place to change your mind about your convictions, but I don't get it. I'm almost thirty, and I've never felt like this before. I've never had this kind of connection. It doesn't happen every day, you know."

"I know." His voice was low and soft. "I haven't had this before, either." He crossed his arms over his broad, muscled chest, his biceps bulging against his uniform sleeves.

"You're willing to walk away from this?" She forced the words out, unsure if she really wanted to hear the answer. Her heart hammered in her throat, and she met his gaze.

"Walk away?" He shook his head and his eyes met hers, snapping in irritation. "Do I look like I'm walking away to you?"

He was angry now, too, and she could feel the tension in the room mounting. She'd rather face him angry than keep butting her head up against his self-controlled calm.

"Then what are you doing?" she demanded.

He dropped his arms and stepped toward her. He pinned her with those fierce blue eyes, emotions battling over his rugged features. "I'm trying really, really hard not to fall head over heels in love with you, Emily. That's what I'm doing."

"And how is that working out for you?" she asked, lifting her chin in defiance.

His answer was in a last step toward her, his strong arm sliding around her waist and pulling her against him so that she could feel the steady beat of his heart against her rib cage. Her hand, planted against his chest, felt the cold metal of his badge next to the heat of his body. His eyes softened as they met hers, and one of his warm hands brushed the hair away from her face and gently caressed her cheek. His eyes stayed fixed on hers as a soft puff of his breath touched her lips.

"I'm failing miserably," he murmured, his voice so low that it rumbled in his chest, against the palms of her hands.

His lips lowered onto hers, and her eyes fluttered closed as he pulled her into a deep, tender kiss that she could feel all the way down to her toes. She reached up, sliding her slender arms around his neck, and when he finally pulled back, looking into her eyes again, she stared up at him breathlessly.

"See?" He released her and took a slow, intentional step away, leaving Emily a little wobbly in the knees.

"Oh," she murmured in reply, planting a hand on the counter for support.

"I'm crazy about you," he said quietly. "More than crazy. I'm in love with you. I love your laugh and your way of seeing things. I love your passion and your mothering instinct that is just so perfect for Cora, or any other children lucky enough to call you Mom. I love you."

She blinked at him. "I love you, too, Greg."

"Which makes it that much worse." His eyes misted, and he looked ready to move toward her again, but he held himself back. "I love you for all the reasons that hold us apart. I can't be a dad, Emily. And I wish with everything in me that I could be."

Emily felt a lump rise in her throat, tears welling up inside of her. "What are you saying, then?"

"I don't know."

"Is this goodbye?" she asked hesitantly.

"No, of course not." He shook his head. "But I might

need some time to—" he stopped, searching for words "—time to get my balance again."

She nodded mutely. His balance? What about hers?

"I'd better get back to the station." He cleared his throat and swallowed, his emotions sliding back behind a mask of professional reserve.

"Okay," she said quietly.

He looked back at Cora in the bassinet, then headed to the front door. "I'll see you," he said, and as quickly as that, he was gone. The door clicked shut behind him, leaving Emily standing there wondering what exactly had just happened.

Chapter Eighteen

The next morning, everything seemed grayer somehow. Greg came into work in a dismal mood. His officers seemed to sense his discontent and steered clear of him, letting him stamp through the station and into his office without so much as a "Hey, Chief!" from any of them. They watched him pass, though, and when he'd slammed the door to his office, the hum of voices started up again.

He'd slept horribly the night before. He kept waking up and staring out at the night sky feeling more alone than he had in a long time. What had changed? Nothing, really. He was still single. He was still the police chief of Haggerston. He was still the son of a woman losing herself to Alzheimer's. The only thing that was different now was that he'd allowed himself to fall in love with the one woman who was least available to him. It was a rookie mistake.

Sitting down at his desk, he turned on his computer and glared angrily out the window at the gray, cloudy day that matched his mood. The air was humid and thick, and the open window did nothing to cool it down inside. He could feel sweat already forming on his brow.

I knew what I was getting into, Lord, so why did I do it?

It hadn't been a choice to fall in love with Emily, and he knew it, although he hadn't exactly fought it tooth and nail, either. He knew she was off-limits. He knew she deeply longed to be a mother, and he knew that he could never be the father of the family she longed for. He knew all of that. He was no fool, but apparently he acted like one from time to time.

I kissed her. That was stupid. He knew he shouldn't have done it. How on earth was pulling her close and letting his lips press into hers going to resolve the issue? It wasn't. It was weakness, pure and simple. He'd done what he'd been longing to do for too long now. How often had he let his mind wander into forbidden territory, wondering what her hair would feel like running through his fingers, or wondering what it would feel like to hold her close against his chest? How often had he wondered what it would be like to look into her eyes and hear her say she loved him?

Well, he'd had the pleasure of hearing those words from her lips, and it had been painful. She loved him back, and there was nothing he could do about it.

Idiot. If he'd left well enough alone, kept a professional distance like he knew he should have done, none of this would have happened, and all he'd be left with would be a lingering crush, something he could deal with quite easily.

He pulled some paperwork in front of him, but his eyes wouldn't focus. Not yet. He ordinarily would go out for coffee in the general office area right about now, but not this morning. He had no desire to make small talk with anyone.

His phone rang, and he welcomed the interruption to his thoughts. Picking it up, he said a curt "Chief Taylor."

"Hello, Chief Taylor, this is Paul Hanson. I'm Emily Shaw's lawyer in the custody case involving the baby from the highway accident of June…" Greg could hear him flipping through pages, looking for a date.

"Yes, yes, I recall it," Greg said. "What can I do for you?"

"You were the officer on the scene when the victim was discovered, weren't you?" the lawyer asked.

"Yes, I was."

"And the victim, Miss Jessica Shaw…she asked you to contact my client and insisted that her baby be placed with her, is that correct?"

"Yes, that's right."

"Was she coherent when she spoke with you?"

"Yes."

"She was badly hurt, though. Are you sure she was coherent?"

"Yes." Greg understood the legal process here. Emily's lawyer was just doing his job, trying to poke holes in his story the same way the opposing counsel would at the hearing. "She knew who she was, she knew she was hurt, she knew her baby would not be able to stay with her. She was very agitated and wanted me to understand that her baby must go to Emily Shaw and no one else."

"Good."

He could hear a pen scratching on the other end.

"Are you willing to testify to that?"

"Absolutely." Greg leaned back in his chair with a squeak. "I'll testify to that. I also know Emily Shaw personally, and I've watched her in a caregiver position with the baby. I'm not a professional witness in that capacity, but if you think it would help, I can testify to her patience and constant love and devotion to Cora, too. She's a good mother. She deserves to stay with this baby now that they've bonded."

"Perfect." He could hear the smile in the lawyer's voice, and he drew the word out with satisfaction. "Just a reminder, the hearing is tomorrow at ten a.m. You'll be there?"

"I sure will."

"Thanks, Chief."

Greg hung up the phone and pursed his lips in thought. He remembered that desperate mother, her face half covered in blood, her eyes frantic as she struggled to breathe. She'd been afraid and unable to even turn toward her baby, but the tiny cries from the backseat had been constant. He felt as if he owed something to that poor woman, the woman whose life had been ebbing away, but her heart had still been with her tiny infant. That mother deserved more than to be forgotten, to have her struggle swept away in court proceedings.

I have one more day. He glanced at the calendar on his desktop. Getting court orders and the like had taken up a lot of time, but there was still enough time to sort out the rest of Jessica's story. At least he hoped it was enough.

Picking up his phone, he dialed Benny's number at his desk.

"Chief?" Benny said, picking up.

"Hi, Benny. I plan to make a little visit to our senator friend. Do me a favor and find out where he'll be tonight. I'd like to have a little surprise chat with him, without giving him the chance to buff up his story."

"Gotcha." Greg could hear the rattle of computer keys. "I'll get it for you in a few minutes, sir."

Greg took a deep breath and stood up. This felt better.

He'd do something useful, get to the end of this mystery surrounding Jessica Shaw, and maybe when he did that, he could close the door on this whole situation and get back to some semblance of normal life again.

Emily stood in her kitchen facing her two best friends. Cora lay contentedly in Nina's arms, looking up at her dangling silver earrings in awe. Beth sat at the kitchen table, munching on a bowl of trail mix. The lights were on inside, making up for the dismal cloud outdoors. It looked as if it might want to rain again, and as Emily stared out the window, she could see the wind picking up, rustling the leaves of the apple tree, whisking a welcome breeze inside.

"Are you ready for the hearing?" Nina asked.

"As ready as I'll ever be. I met with my lawyer this morning, and we went over what to expect. Basically, he just said to be myself."

"Good advice," Beth said with a nod.

Emily sighed. "I guess I can't do much else, but I'd really rather have some sort of strategy so I felt like I was doing something."

Nina chuckled. "I get that. That's very type A of you."

"Anyone who sees you with Cora will know you belong together," Beth said. She leaned over and tweaked one of Cora's toes, making the baby smile. "Will Greg be there?"

Emily nodded. "He's a witness."

"Yes, yes." Nina laughed. "We aren't asking if he's coming as a witness. Will he be there for you?"

Emily was silent. Would he? She had no idea where they stood right now. The kettle started to whistle on the stove, and she distracted herself with getting down the teapot from the cupboard above the stove and reaching for the tea leaves and strainer. It was a hot and humid day, but it still felt like a day that needed tea, if only going through the motions for comfort.

"Emily?" Beth asked softly.

"I don't know." Emily felt tears misting her eyes. "It's complicated." She put the pot down with a soft clatter, then covered it with her hands. The last thing she needed was to break her favorite teapot today, too.

"Complicated how?" Nina pressed.

Cora started to fuss, and Emily walked over to take the baby from Nina's arms, pulling Cora in close for a cuddle. The infant instantly settled, happy to be in Emily's arms, and Nina went to take over with the tea.

"He came over yesterday afternoon, and he…we…" How was she supposed to explain this?

"What happened?" Beth asked. "Did you break up?"

"We were never together." Emily laughed bitterly. "How could we break up?"

The other two women were silent, the only sound the clink of spoon against teapot as Nina added tea leaves, and Emily's eyes wandered out the window where some drizzling rain was starting to fall.

"He said he loves me," Emily finally said softly.

"Wow!" Beth burst out. "That's good, right?"

Emily looked back at her friend with her large pregnant belly and twinkling, expectant eyes. Beth had been married since she graduated from university at twenty-two. She had no idea what it was like to be single at thirty, or to face anything completely alone. She'd always had Howard, either as a boyfriend or a husband. She couldn't blame Beth for her happiness, though.

"It doesn't change anything. He doesn't want kids, and I do. Isn't that the same thing that's been between us the whole time?" Emily looked down at Cora with her big blue eyes and pudgy little hands. They were at an impasse.

"You are both ridiculously stubborn," Nina said.

"I said that before," Beth agreed.

"Actually, he's the ridiculously stubborn one," Emily replied. "It isn't my place to change his mind, but he wants to be with us so badly—he just won't allow himself the pleasure."

"Good grief. Do you love him?"

Emily looked at them mutely, and Beth nodded. "Of course you do."

"There's nothing to do," Emily said. "I knew I was doing this on my own from the beginning. That is no surprise to me."

"You aren't alone." Beth stretched as far as she could past her belly and put her hand over Emily's. "You'll always have us. Cora is going to be one loved little girl, and Auntie Beth plans to be a big part of her life."

Nina grinned. "Don't forget about Auntie Nina. Someone has to teach that girl to shop."

Emily couldn't help but smile. "I can do this."

"Of course you can," Nina agreed, carrying the pot to the table. "You're strong, capable, loving and everything that Cora could ever dream of in a mom. You'll go in there tomorrow, hold your head high and show the judge what a perfect choice Jessica made."

"That's the plan."

Emily looked down at Cora, whose eyes were drooping tiredly. She leaned her plump cheek against Emily's shirt, nestling in closer to drift off to sleep. She was getting bigger in her arms now. She remembered not too long ago when the wee thing fit along her forearm comfortably, but now she needed two hands to hold her.

She was growing, and she was thriving. More than that, Emily was growing, too—personally and spiritually.

Tomorrow, she would go into the hearing with a prayer in her heart and ask to be allowed to keep Cora in her life. Would it be enough? Only God knew. All she could do was pray that tonight wasn't the last night that little Cora would sleep in this house.

Chapter Nineteen

That evening, Greg pulled up in front of a large mansion in Rimrock, the wealthiest section of Billings. It was hard to see much detail through the foggy rain, but from what he could tell, it was a three-story affair, brick with white trim. The windows glowed cheerfully, the light from chandeliers sparkling through the cracks in heavy drapery. As he parked his cruiser and turned off the engine, he sent up a quick prayer.

He'd been praying the entire drive from their little town of Haggerston to Billings, a two-hour commute. It was the same highway that Jessica had driven and died on all those weeks ago, and as he drove he'd poured his heart out to his Father. The solitude was what he needed—solitude and a mission. He needed to do something, fix something. Anything.

No, not anything, he thought to himself. *This.*

Was he wasting his time with this visit? He didn't know. There was no crime committed for the senator to be wary of, at least no crime that they knew of. There were simply unanswered questions, and the senator may very well not feel like chatting.

Pushing open the door to his cruiser, he plunged

through the rain to the front door and pressed the doorbell. A long, melodious series of chimes rang through the house and he paused, listening. He heard the dead bolt being retracted, and an older woman in a housekeeping uniform opened the door cautiously, peering past a chain.

"Good evening," Greg said. "I'm the chief of police in Haggerston, and I've come to ask Senator Lindgren a few questions."

"Police?" The woman frowned. "One moment, please."

The door shut again; there was the scrape of the chain being removed and a couple of seconds later it opened again to allow him entrance. He stepped into a brightly lit foyer with stone tiles and a vaulted ceiling, a crystal chandelier hanging overhead. The senator paused midway down the spiral staircase as he looked around, a paisley dressing gown tied around his waist. He was a fit man in his fifties with iron-gray hair and a smooth tan.

"How can I help you, Officer?" the senator asked. "Is something wrong?"

"I'm Chief Greg Taylor, Chief of Police in Haggerston. I've come to ask you a few questions. I hope I haven't disturbed you, sir." Greg met the senator's gaze easily.

"Out of your jurisdiction, aren't you, son?" Senator Lindgren smiled evenly, caution edging his tone.

"Sure am," Greg agreed. "I only have a few questions. I was hoping you could help me out with an investigation I'm doing. It shouldn't take long."

The senator seemed to consider for a moment, then he nodded, gesturing toward a room on the main floor. Greg followed his host into a library. It was a cozy room with a gas fireplace, unlit at this time of night, floor-to-ceiling mahogany bookshelves and a bearskin rug on the floor beside several overstuffed leather chairs. It was a comfortable room, a man's room. A humidor for cigars was set to one side, and a collection of antique rifles decorated one wall.

"It must be of some importance to bring you out at this time of night," the senator commented, gesturing for Greg to have a seat.

"Well, there has been a death," Greg said, nodding.

"Who?"

Greg ignored the question. "I was hoping you could tell me a little bit about Jessica Shaw."

The senator narrowed his eyes and pursed his lips. He was taking his time to consider before answering, something people rarely did. Greg was silently impressed with the man's control already.

"What about her?" the senator finally asked.

"Why were you giving her large sums of money monthly?"

Senator Lindgren gave a tight smile and looked past Greg to point behind him. "That is between Miss Shaw and myself."

"Senator, I have no intention of making trouble for you," Greg said, his voice low. "I need to have some questions answered, and that is as far as this needs to go. However, if you aren't going to cooperate with me, I could contact the Billings police to aid me in this. That would get complicated. And official."

Senator Lindgren sighed, his eyes suddenly looking very tired. He was getting somewhere. Taking advantage of a sign of weakness, Greg pressed on. "Did you have her followed?"

"Yes, but that is much worse than it sounds." The senator shook his head. "I simply had a private detective ensure that she…was doing what she said she would be doing."

"Which was?" Greg slid his hands along the smooth leather armrests, watching the older man's expression turn from exhaustion to wariness once more.

"She was going home."

"I realize that," Greg said. "And you wanted to make sure she went home?"

The senator nodded. "Yes."

"Why?"

"It was good for her."

"And for you."

"Yes, and for me." The senator leaned forward, resting his elbows on his knees. "Son, some things are personal."

Greg regarded the older man dubiously. He was smooth, practiced and not easily intimidated. He'd been in politics too long to be susceptible to these interview techniques. He could question and barter all night, and he'd get very little out of the man. It was time to level with him.

"Senator, Jessica Shaw is dead."

Senator Lindgren blinked twice, swallowed, then shook his head. "What?"

"She's dead."

"When? How?"

"The same night she drove back to Haggerston."

The shock was certainly real, and Greg leaned forward, locking eyes with the older man. "Who was she, Senator? Was she your mistress?"

"Mistress?" the older man barked out. "Good grief, man, no!"

The vehemence of the man's response was a surprise to Greg. He was inclined to believe him, as little sense as that made. Greg waited silently, but when he got nothing else out of the man, he said, "Then who was Jessica Shaw to you?"

"She was my daughter." Senator Lindgren stood up and rubbed his hands over his face. He looked distraught, but not grief-stricken, and Greg rolled this new piece of information over in his mind. His daughter? But wasn't there an Uncle Hank back in Haggerston who was grieving the loss of his only daughter?

"Forgive me for being dubious," Greg said slowly. "But are you sure?"

The older man smiled wanly. "Do I look like a man who would accept paternity lightly?"

"So you were giving her money to help with the baby?" Greg asked.

"No, I was giving her money to ensure she'd go away," he retorted. "I had an affair with her mother thirty years ago. Her mother was briefly separated from her husband, and I met her at an opera. It was a short-lived fling, which ended when she went back to her husband."

"And your wife?" Greg asked.

"Knows nothing of it. It was my one indiscretion. I've never been unfaithful since."

A lie. Even Mrs Lindgren knew better than that, but this wasn't about the sanctity of his marriage, so Greg let it go.

"So Jessica was a child born from an affair." Greg frowned. "Did her mother tell her husband?"

"I have no idea." Senator Lindgren shrugged. "That was her business. She said she didn't want anyone to know what she'd done, and that suited me just fine."

"So when did Jessica contact you?"

"A few months ago. She was pregnant. She'd learned about me from her mother a few years ago, and she decided to come and meet her biological father." There was a shade of disgust in his voice as he said it, as if the thought were ridiculous at best.

"You didn't want a relationship with her?" Greg pushed himself to his feet and walked toward the fireplace thoughtfully.

"A relationship?" The senator laughed bitterly. "I don't have children for a reason, Chief."

"Which is?"

"I don't want them. They complicate things. They're good for politics only when they behave perfectly. I didn't take that risk in my career."

Greg looked up at some old paintings of Lindgren men of yore along the wall. It was hard to believe that the old senator didn't want to sire an heir of his own, but apparently he didn't.

"So why did you have her followed?"

"We agreed on a price. I'd pay her, and she'd go back home and stay there. I just wanted to make sure she'd made good on her end of the deal." He rubbed his hands together as if he were cold, then plunged them into the pockets of his dressing gown. He looked irritably toward the door, no doubt wishing Greg would leave through it.

"You had no idea she was dead."

"No."

"You don't seem terribly broken up about that fact."

"Should I be?" The man shook his head in exasperation. "I barely knew her. She was a starving artist looking for a handout. She didn't feel anything more for me than I felt for her."

"Are you sure?"

"She wanted money."

"Did she ask for money?"

"No." The senator frowned and hunched up his shoulders, then sighed. "No, she didn't ask for money, but she didn't turn it down, either."

"Is it possible she really did want a relationship with her biological father?"

"That wasn't possible. My wife didn't know about her. I couldn't let the public know about her. I paid her to go away, and she took the money and left."

He rejected her. Greg suddenly had an image in his mind of a pregnant young woman reaching out to her biological father, hoping for some special connection now that she was estranged from her family. The senator didn't care about her one way or another; he just wanted her to go away and leave his charmed life alone. Hurt, rejected, insulted, she took the money and headed back home. Only she never made it.

"And the baby?" Greg asked.

"What about it?" the senator asked tiredly.

"Do you know who the father was?"

He shook his head. "Some fellow artist, I imagine. I have no idea. She told me at one point that the father didn't want anything to do with her." He shook his head sadly. "Neither did I. She was better off at home."

"Thank you, Senator." Greg gave the older man his most professional smile. "I appreciate your candor."

"I don't have to stress how much I'll value your discretion," he said, a smooth smile returning to his face. "I can be an influential friend to have, Chief."

"I'll be very discreet." Greg returned the smile. "But don't count on my vote next election."

Chapter Twenty

Outside the judge's office, Greg sat on a bench along the wall, waiting. He held his hat in his hands, rolling it end over end. He would be called in as a witness at some point soon. The scent of the lemon floor polish combined with that unique courthouse smell was comforting. He'd spent many a morning in a situation like this over the years, waiting in full uniform to give his testimony about a case. It wasn't that he didn't know what to expect. He knew exactly what to expect, and in this case he also knew the judge personally. Judge Willis would be fair and impartial. She always was. Emily was the part that made it personal. Both Emily and Cora, to be precise.

He heard movement inside, and then the door opened. Steve and Sara came out together. Steve looked down at Greg and frowned.

"Greg Taylor?" His voice held a slightly high-pitched ring to it.

"Hi, Steve." Greg wasn't in a mood to play this game. He stood up, enjoying the fact that he was four inches taller than Steve, forcing him to look up.

"How are you doing, man?" Steve asked, reaching out to shake his hand. "This is my wife, Sara."

"Pleased to meet you." He shook her hand in turn. Steve's refusal to use his professional title this morning wasn't lost on him. Steve had always been the manipulative type, using subtlety to gain an edge.

"Well, this should be over soon," Steve said with a smile. "When we're done here, you should come by our place for a little dinner with our girls."

He was already mentally celebrating, Greg realized. That wasn't good news, and he personally resented that Cora was silently being lumped in with "his girls."

"Is it over already?" Greg asked.

"No, no. They'll want to hear from you still, I'm sure." Steve shrugged and grinned. "But good to see you, Greg. We're just going to go call the girls and see how they're doing."

As Steve and Sara moved on down the hall, Greg looked after them, narrowing his eyes. Smooth. That was the best way to describe Steve. Much like Senator Lindgren. He knew how to position himself above other people and how to keep himself there. Less subtle men used open bullying, but Steve was no better than a common bully. He was just better at masking his motives. The question was, what was actually lurking under that smooth veneer?

As Emily stepped out of the room, Cora held close in her arms, she looked deflated. Her beige pantsuit made her look more conservative than she generally looked, the only splash of color a pink blouse that peeked from beneath the jacket. Her hair was pulled away from her face in a bun, and there were tears in her eyes when she slowly turned and looked at Greg. She gave him a small smile.

"Hi," he said. "How's it going in there?"

"I don't know. They're basically saying that I'm emotionally unstable because of the call I made to Steve after I was followed. It was recorded. Oh, and apparently I'm a workaholic. Being a single mom is being used against me, too. I seem to lose by default."

"Steve's an idiot" was Greg's response. "I don't like him."

"The judge seems to."

"Come on." Greg took her arm and guided her down the hall. He could see Steve and Sara talking on a cell phone near the door for better reception. Turning to Emily, he said quietly, "I have the rest of Jessica's story."

"Oh?" She frowned, looking up at him. That seemed to break through her fog, and she focused on his face, her eyes sharpening.

"I made a visit to Senator Lindgren last night. We identified him as the one giving your cousin large sums of money monthly."

"The senator..." Emily frowned uncertainly. "Then she was having an affair with him?"

"No, he was her *father*."

Emily shook her head. "That can't be. Uncle Hank is her father."

"Hank raised her. Hank and June had a brief separation, and during that time Jessica was conceived. I doubt Hank ever knew that Jessica wasn't his. Maybe he didn't care. Jessica discovered the truth somehow and went to talk to her biological father."

"Was he trying to support the baby?" Emily asked.

"He was paying her to go away."

From across the foyer, Greg could hear Steve talking to his daughters in exaggeratedly cheerful tones. The door opened to the outside, letting in the sound of a passing garbage truck, then closed, muffling it again.

"Really?" Emily's eyes met his. "She was coming

back here because her own father wanted nothing to do with her?"

"Neither did the father of her baby. Apparently, he was another artist who didn't want to be a dad." Those words almost stuck in his throat. It seemed as if there were a lot of men out there not wanting to be fathers.

"So why did she choose me?" Emily looked up at him questioningly.

"Steve is smooth, Em, but he's an awful lot like that senator. He smiles and says the right things, but his motives…they are eerily alike. The senator didn't want children. Steve does. Besides that difference, they carry themselves the same way—in perfect self-interest. They don't care who they railroad to get their way. Frankly? I think Jessica knew exactly why she chose you. You're the right one to raise Cora."

Emily looked down at the baby in her arms and held her closer, resting her cheek against the soft baby curls. She closed her eyes, and he could see the struggle it was to keep her emotions under control. "What do I do?"

"Go in there and show the judge that Jessica was right. You're not married. You're an excellent teacher, and you're a loving mother. Stand up for all the single, working moms out there. Mine worked her fingers to the bone. This isn't about staying at home or working—it's about being a loving mom."

She looked up at him, her big eyes filled with apprehension. She was pale—probably hadn't eaten that morning from being too nervous. She blinked back tears and gave him a faint smile. There was something about that soft smile that lit something inside of him. He didn't care what it meant for his job or for his future with Emily. *No one* was going to push her around and break her heart. Greg bent down and pressed his lips gently against her warm forehead. "It's not over yet, Emily," he murmured. "Go fight for your baby."

And if she was getting worn out in the fight, he was right behind her—fresh and ready.

An hour later, as everyone filed out, Greg eased next to Emily, his strong arm brushing up against her. He bent toward her ever so slightly, and Emily had to stop herself from leaning into his arms. But she didn't need to complicate his life anymore.

She had won custody. She'd do this on her own with the help of her family. Emily looked up into his warm blue eyes, and he smiled.

"You did it." His voice was soft and low, meant for her ears only.

"Thanks to you, Greg." She beamed up at him. "Really, thank you. You have no idea how much this means to me."

She looked down at Cora with the joyful certainty that they were going home together. They weren't going to be separated. She was Cora's mom!

"You deserve it. You two belong together." He gently ran a finger down Cora's tiny hand. "Now you can relax and enjoy this." He leaned over and put a kiss on Cora's downy head. "Bye-bye, Sweet pea."

"Greg?"

"Yes?" Greg looked down at her, a deep sadness welling in his eyes.

"Is *this* goodbye?"

"It better not be." He reached out and put his warm, strong hand against her cheek, and she couldn't help but lean into his touch. "Go celebrate."

"Okay."

He took a deep breath, then he gave her a nod, as if steeling himself. Emily felt a sudden wave of sadness as he pulled away from her, heading off in the opposite direction. If only she could have it all, but sometimes that wasn't possible. Pulling her eyes away from Greg's broad, strong back, Emily headed toward the outside door. Cora was up on her shoulder looking around with her bright, curious eyes. As Emily pushed open the heavy glass door, an older lady pulled it open the rest of the way for them and looked at Cora with a grandmotherly smile on her face.

"She's beautiful," the lady said.

"Thank you." Emily turned toward her, flashing a radiant smile. "This is my daughter."

Chapter Twenty-One

That evening, Greg lay on his couch at home, one arm over his eyes. It had been a long day. He'd been up late the night before, driving the two hours back to Haggerston after his visit with Senator Lindgren, and then he'd been up early for the hearing. Now he felt the comfort of his couch against his tired back, but his mind wouldn't stop turning.

Jessica Shaw hadn't been the wild child he'd assumed she was. He liked being proven wrong in things like that, but another part of her story was nagging at him: her rejection. She'd been upset coming back to her hometown, and her emotional state probably had a lot to do with the accident. She just hadn't been as alert as she could have been—a split-second decision made a split second too late. She'd been rejected by her boyfriend, but people recovered from breakups. The rejection that probably ate away at her was the parental one. Her own father had rejected her, given her money to go away and leave him alone.

Greg sighed. He'd lost his dad, too, but he'd never doubted that his father loved him. There was a difference there. He could remember sitting with his dad on the step of their little house, looking out at the sidewalk. His dad would just sit there with him in silence, for the most part. They liked to watch the shadows lengthen. There were times even now when he'd sit on the step to his house and look out at the drive that led to the road. It wasn't the same view as when he was young, but if he closed his eyes he could almost feel the solid warmth of his father sitting next to him.

The phone rang, and Greg reached blindly for it and picked it up.

"Hello?"

"Chief?" It was Fran. "We've got a bit of a situation here. Your mom is pretty upset."

Greg swung his legs around and sat up, blinking himself back into wakefulness. "What's happening?"

"She won't calm down. It's been getting worse lately, Chief. What would you like us to do?"

In the background he could hear his mother's voice rising above the din. She was afraid. He could hear the fear in her voice, and he rammed his feet into his shoes.

"I'm on my way," he said. "I'll be there soon."

"Okay. Thanks."

Greg hung up the phone and immediately dialed again. "Hi, Emily? I wonder if you'd be willing to do me that favor?"

Emily pulled into the nursing-home parking lot. The sun had set, and Cora snoozed comfortably in her car seat. With the pressure gone now, Emily felt as if she was riding a wave of love and thankfulness. They belonged together—the court had ruled in her favor. On Monday, she already had an appointment with her lawyer to start the process of legally adopting Cora.

Greg stood by the doors to the nursing home, waiting for her. When he saw her drive in, he raised his hand in a wave and walked in the direction she turned to park. He met her at her door and held it open while she hopped out.

"Is she okay?" Emily asked.

"Not really. She's upset. I convinced them to wait for us before they sedate her. I want to at least try."

Emily nodded and pulled open the rear door, leaning in to pull out Cora, still asleep in her car seat.

"We should hurry." He reached toward the car seat. "Do you want a hand?"

"No, thanks." She grinned up at him. "I'm okay."

He smiled back, and she sensed he understood. As they made their way back toward the front door, she tried not to lean into his warm arm. There was no need to make being just friends harder than it had to be. He pulled the door open for her, and as they stepped inside Emily could hear the cries of an old woman. She wasn't angry; she was weeping, frightened, and her heart immediately melted. Looking up at Greg, she saw tears mist his eyes.

The nurse met them at the door.

"You're here. Thank goodness."

"Fran," Emily said quietly. "Would you hold Cora for me for a few minutes?"

Fran smiled tenderly down at the baby. "My pleasure. She and I will just wait for you here in the hall."

Emily turned to Greg uncertainly. "What do you want me to do?" This was his mother, and she knew how desperately he wanted to help, but she wasn't sure what he even wanted from her.

"Just go in first. She's more comfortable with women. She won't remember you, but I think she'll be calmer with you here."

Emily nodded and tapped softly on the door.

"Hello?" she called.

The sobbing lessened, and as Emily came into the room she saw the little woman on her bed, her legs pulled up against her chest and her gray hair hanging down into her reddened eyes. An orderly stood to the side, but he wasn't bothering her at all—just standing there, making sure she didn't hurt herself.

"Where's my mommy?" Greg's mother whispered. "I want my mommy and daddy."

She'd slipped back years to her childhood, and Emily felt a wave of pity. She moved slowly toward the bed, then sat down on the edge. Greg came in after, but he hung back.

"What's your name?" Emily asked softly.

"Laura."

"I'm Emily."

Laura sniffed and wiped her nose against her hand. "It's dark," she said.

"I know. Are you afraid of the dark?"

Laura nodded. "I don't know where my mommy and daddy are."

"They aren't far away," Emily said. "They'll be here soon. Don't worry."

"Who's that?"

Emily glanced back at Greg. He stood there looking at his mother, his eyes filled with sadness.

"That's my friend Greg. He knows your daddy really well. He's come here to be with you until your daddy can come."

"Oh." Laura looked up hopefully. "You know my daddy?"

Greg nodded, swallowing hard. "Yes, I know him well. Are you okay…Laura?" He stumbled over his mother's first name, but he took a step forward. Emily stood up, making room for him.

"I'm okay." Her voice still quavered. "I don't like the dark."

"Oh, it isn't so bad," Greg said softly. "Did you know that even in the dark, there are stars to light our way?"

He looked over at Emily, a small smile on his lips, and she felt her own eyes misting with tears. It was a small thing, but if her own father's tenderness when she had been afraid of the dark could help Greg's mother, she was grateful.

"So it isn't so scary, then?" Laura asked hopefully.

"That's right." He sat down next to her. "It's not so scary. There is always a twinkling star looking down at you. That's why God made them—so you'd never be in the dark."

His mother wiped her hair out of her eyes and then looked up at Greg hopefully. "My daddy hugs me when I'm scared."

"Do you...?" Greg looked at her tentatively. "Do you want a hug from me?"

She nodded, her eyes still brimming with unshed tears. Greg carefully put his arms around her, and she leaned her gray head against his strong chest. Tears welled up in his eyes, and his chin quivered. He gently laid his cheek against the top of her hair and let out a deep sigh.

"It's going to be okay," he said softly. "Why don't you close your eyes now, and I'll hold you while you go to sleep?"

She obediently closed her eyes. She was exhausted, and as he held her, rocking her gently back and forth, he softly hummed that old familiar tune: *twinkle, twinkle, little star. How I wonder what you are...*

Emily moved back to the door, leaving the two of them alone. Taking Cora back from Fran with a smile of thanks, she stood in the doorway, watching Greg as he softly sang his mother to sleep. Emily watched him for a long time, and when he finally laid her down on her bed, he kissed her forehead tenderly and turned back toward Emily silently.

They walked back down the hallway together, neither of them saying a word to each other.

"Thanks for coming, Chief," Fran said before they left. "You're a good son."

As they stepped outside, the warm summer air engulfed them with the scent of flowers and the soft hum of insects. Greg looked down at her as they slowly walked back across the parking lot.

"Thank you," he said quietly. "Thank you so much."

Emily put her arm through his and rested her head against his shoulder. "It was all you, Greg. She needed you, whether she knew who you were or not."

"She wanted her daddy." Greg stopped walking and looked down at Emily. "Did you hear that?"

Emily felt the old sadness welling up inside of her. "I know. Dads are important. I'm not pressuring you, Greg. I understand."

He chuckled softly. "I don't think you do." He guided her toward her SUV and waited while she put Cora into the backseat and lowered the window halfway. When she closed the door and turned toward him, he cleared his throat. "I always thought that losing my dad the way I did was the worst thing that could happen to a child. But then I started trying to find out Jessica's story. She was looking for her biological father, and when she found him he didn't want her. He rejected her. That loss— that was worse. I know how much my dad loved me, but Jessica knew the hard truth about the senator. He not only didn't love her, but was willing to pay her to get rid of her."

Emily nodded sadly. The warm breeze picked up, ruffling her blouse against her arms, and she ran her fingers through her hair to keep it out of her eyes.

"I know," she said softly.

"I've been trying to protect Cora from going through what I went through, but maybe I should follow my heart instead, and protect her from what Jessica experienced."

Emily blinked, looking up at him in surprise. "What are you saying, Greg?"

"I'm saying I want to be a family. I want to take care of you two, love you, grow old with you, be there to walk our daughter down the aisle. I'm not her biological father, but I could make up for that."

Emily felt tears rising in her eyes as she imagined a life with Greg, raising Cora together. He stepped closer, looking down into her face with uncertain, searching eyes.

"But you have to understand," he went on carefully. "My job is dangerous. Something might happen to me. You could marry someone else and—"

"And what?" She laughed softly. "Wish I'd married you all along?"

A smile tugged at the corners of his lips. "I love you, Emily."

He lowered his lips onto hers, and she closed her eyes and melted into his kiss. His arms wound around her, and he pulled her close so that she stood on the tips of her toes, her arms twined around his neck. When he pulled back, he touched her nose with his, smiling.

"I love you, too, Greg." She swallowed nervously. "Now ask me properly."

Greg laughed softly, the sound reverberating through his strong chest. "Emily Shaw, will you marry me?"

"Yes!" She nodded, laughter bubbling up inside of her. "Yes, I'll marry you!"

As his lips came down over hers again, she closed her eyes in the starlight, feeling as if the entire world was swirling around her.

Up above the world so high, like a diamond in the sky. Her happiness was complete.

* * * * *

*If you enjoyed this story by Patricia Johns,
be sure to check out the other books this month
from Love Inspired!*

Dear Reader,

This book emerged when I was wishing for another baby. I think a lot of women can identify with that whisper of longing, and what's easier than having a baby dropped off on your doorstep? If you're a mom, you just burst out laughing at that line. Tiny babies have a way of taking over your life regardless of how they arrive.

I'm a novelist who always has a book in process. We live on the Canadian prairies where the winters are long and frigid, and the summers are hot and buggy. It's absolutely perfect because I always have an excellent excuse to stay in and write.

I'd love to get to know you, too! I'm writing for you, and connecting with my readers makes that circle complete. So come by my blog at http://patriciajohnsromance. com, or look me up on Facebook under Patricia Johns Romance. I'll be the one hammering away on a novel and sharing quirky tidbits from my life. Drop me a line—I'll be sure to answer!

Patricia

Questions for Discussion

1. Emily loves kids, but isn't able to have a baby of her own. Have you ever prayed for something that seemed entirely hopeless?

2. Greg was bullied as a child, but he's able to help the son of his childhood bully through his own tough adolescent adjustments. How do you think bullying can affect a person's life, even years later? How might God use that painful experience for good?

3. Greg's mother suffers from Alzheimer's, and has forgotten who he is. Have you ever felt abandoned by a parent? Is it possible to feel orphaned at the loss of a parent, even as an adult?

4. Greg is in the position of caring for his ailing mother, and when she slips back into her childhood in her mind, he's finally able to hold his mother and give her a hug. What are some of the challenges of caring for an aging or ailing parent? What are some of the blessings in disguise?

5. When Cora's mother is killed in a car accident, Steve and Sara want to raise the baby. Do you think there are times when good intentions end up causing more pain?

6. Emily's father told her that God gave us stars so we'd never be in the dark. What pinpricks of hope do you find in tough situations?

7. Emily tells Greg that now that she's tasted motherhood, she can't be happy without a child of her own. This is a dividing point for them. Do you have anything in your life that you wouldn't be willing to give up for love?

8. Emily's best friend Beth is married and pregnant. Emily is happy for her friend, but it isn't always easy. Do you ever struggle with conflicting emotions when a dear friend achieves the very thing you've been longing for?

9. Emily doesn't want Cora to grow up without a close and connected extended family. What benefits does a supportive extended family offer? What is your extended family like?

10. Emily longs to raise Cora, but she isn't the baby's closest biological relative. Should this matter? What do you think is the most important quality in a mother?

11. Greg doesn't want to be a father because he's afraid his job is too dangerous and he doesn't want to be killed in the line of duty and leave a family behind to fend for themselves. Have you ever made a difficult decision because you wanted to protect the people you love?

12. Emily's cousin Jessica attempts to contact her biological father only to be rejected by him. He is more concerned with his career than his daughter. How

does your father's acceptance or rejection of you affect your self-image? How does your Heavenly Father rectify some of those hurts?

COMING NEXT MONTH from Love Inspired®
AVAILABLE JULY 23, 2013

THE BACHELOR BAKER
The Heart of Main Street
Carolyne Aarsen
When a traditional man and a career-minded woman work together in her bakery, they'll find love isn't always a piece of cake.

HEALING HEARTS
Caring Canines
Margaret Daley
Both Abbey Harris and Dominic Winters long for a second chance at love, and it'll take two adorable dogs and a sweet little girl to bring them together.

THE SOLDIER'S SWEETHEART
Serendipity Sweethearts
Deb Kastner
On the verge of losing her family's store, the last thing Samantha Howell needs is ex-soldier Will Davenport seeking a job. But he might just be the answer to her prayers....

ROCKY COAST ROMANCE
Holiday Harbor
Mia Ross
When feisty reporter Bree Farrell lands in the small town of Holiday Harbor, she never expects to fall in love with the town—or its handsome mayor.

BRIDE WANTED
Renee Andrews
Troy Lee has been searching for his one true love for years, and he thinks he might have finally found her. But can he trust his heart to a beautiful city slicker with a secret?

DADDY NEXT DOOR
Carol Voss
When a widowed mom flees to her grandmother's cottage to start over, she finds new hope where she least expects it—the single dad next door.

Look for these and other Love Inspired books wherever books are sold, including most bookstores, supermarkets, discount stores and drugstores.

REQUEST YOUR FREE BOOKS!

2 FREE INSPIRATIONAL NOVELS
PLUS 2
FREE
MYSTERY GIFTS

Love Inspired®

YES! Please send me 2 FREE Love Inspired® novels and my 2 FREE mystery gifts (gifts are worth about $10). After receiving them, if I don't wish to receive any more books, I can return the shipping statement marked "cancel." If I don't cancel, I will receive 6 brand new novels every month and be billed just $4.74 per book in the U.S. or $5.24 per book in Canada. That's a saving of at least 21% off the cover price. It's quite a bargain! Shipping and handling is just 50¢ per book in the U.S. and 75¢ per book in Canada.* I understand that accepting the 2 free books and gifts places me under no obligation to buy anything. I can always return a shipment and cancel at any time. Even if I never buy another book, the two free books and gifts are mine to keep forever.

105/305 IDN F47Y

Name	(PLEASE PRINT)

Address	Apt. #

City	State/Prov.	Zip/Postal Code

Signature (if under 18, a parent or guardian must sign)

Mail to the Harlequin® Reader Service:
IN U.S.A.: P.O. Box 1867, Buffalo, NY 14240-1867
IN CANADA: P.O. Box 609, Fort Erie, Ontario L2A 5X3

**Are you a subscriber to Love Inspired books
and want to receive the larger-print edition?
Call 1-800-873-8635 or visit www.ReaderService.com.**

* Terms and prices subject to change without notice. Prices do not include applicable taxes. Sales tax applicable in N.Y. Canadian residents will be charged applicable taxes. Offer not valid in Quebec. This offer is limited to one order per household. Not valid for current subscribers to Love Inspired books. All orders subject to credit approval. Credit or debit balances in a customer's account(s) may be offset by any other outstanding balance owed by or to the customer. Please allow 4 to 6 weeks for delivery. Offer available while quantities last.

Your Privacy—The Harlequin® Reader Service is committed to protecting your privacy. Our Privacy Policy is available online at www.ReaderService.com or upon request from the Harlequin Reader Service.

We make a portion of our mailing list available to reputable third parties that offer products we believe may interest you. If you prefer that we not exchange your name with third parties, or if you wish to clarify or modify your communication preferences, please visit us at www.ReaderService.com/consumerschoice or write to us at Harlequin Reader Service Preference Service, P.O. Box 9062, Buffalo, NY 14269. Include your complete name and address.

LII3R

Both Abbey Harris and Dominic Winters long for a second
chance at love, and it'll take two adorable dogs and a sweet
little girl to bring them together.

Healing Hearts
by Margaret Daley

Available August 2013
wherever Love Inspired books are sold.

www.LoveInspiredBooks.com

LI87830